Assassins: Into the Light

By Anthony Brenes

Assassins: Into the Light

By Anthony Brenes

Contents

Chapter 1: Into the Light

In a busy market square sat an old man enjoying his morning cup of tea only to realize that there was something wrong with its taste. It wasn't before long that he found himself entering the pearly gates. Cullen couldn't believe he pulled off his first job as a professional Assassin. Sure, he had no idea if the guy was innocent or not, but he earned a hefty sack of gold.

"Cullen, wake up you need to resume your training!" shouted Master Flint. The middle aged man of 50 looked down at him with his grey eyes, which matched his mostly grey and brown hair. He scratched his beard, which surprisingly still stayed brown.

"Sorry, Master, I was just dreaming about my first solo job," replied Cullen as he yawned and rubbed his eyes.

The Assassins were a society of killers for hire who lived on their own planet, which has been their base ever since their beginning many millennia ago. They were not without their rules, but one thing for sure was how they did not question who their target was as long as they were paid. The main rules stated that the Assassins were no one's ally, never chose their own target, never killed another Assassin, obeyed their Masters, and only killed their target. Besides that an Assassin's life was their own. Procreation wasn't looked down upon at all, but their progeny could not be Assassins.

"Now show me your combat skills so I can assess your readiness to face our next target. If I feel you are ready, then I will only step in if you fail to kill your target. You are 24 now. If you can take out this target on your own, your training will be complete," explained Master Flint.

"Alright, I'm not going to hold back, Master, since you never do."

Cullen suddenly disappeared in a puff of smoke, keeping in mind that he could only maintain his technique for 20 seconds. Before making any moves, he waited to see if his Master could sense where he was. Flint looked to his right instead of keeping his eyes forward, which gave Cullen the idea of advancing towards Flint's left. Cullen went to sweep Flint's leg, but he simply jumped up and punched his pupil in the face. Cullen staggered back, while readying himself for the follow up with his stealth, now deactivated from being hit.

"Very good, Cullen, I could not sense your presence until I felt the air move from your kick. Strengthen the swiftness of your kick and it will take a Master a caliber above my own to be the wiser."

"Thank you, Master, I take it your compliment means that I can solo this mission."

"Absolutely!" confirmed Flint with a nod of approval.

The trainees who have reached Cullen's level have been with their Masters since the age of 13. Every assassin chose both a primary and secondary skill set to develop including open combat, stealth, alchemy, and trap making.

Every assassin also chose a favored weapon to train. Cullen did not actually have an affinity for being an assassin, but eventually became one of the more promising young users of stealth. On the other hand it turned out that he was a natural at alchemy because his love of nature and knack for finding rare herbs. His weapon of choice was a curved dagger, which he would conceal on his person. Each weapon was not only that, they were living beings. On the Assassin's planet, Kelvar, lived special animals that had the ability to speak to their partners through telepathy or out loud and transform into weapon form. Cullen's weapon was named Fang, a grey wolf from the most dangerous forest area on the planet.

There was a cool breeze filling the night air of the city at around 9 o'clock. The target, visiting one of his mistresses, stayed at one of the biggest hotels on the planet Lexon. It was known as one of the premier gambling, luxury, and vacation spots in the universe. The target enjoyed the safety of heavy security on his floor, right outside his room. Lucky for Cullen, one of the waiters decided to take a short smoke break. He snuck in after the waiter opened the door and stole a uniform from the locker room. Once fully disguised, Cullen played the part of the waiter for a few hours, until he heard that his target had ordered room service. All he had to do was make a deal with the waitress who would complete that order so that he could accompany her to the room. He offered his help, so she wouldn't have to make two trips.

On the way to the target's room, Cullen felt nervous. Not because he was killing someone, but because he had already killed his share of targets. He knew that completing his training would mean that he could have more freedoms in his life. He could live anywhere off of Kelvar, choose his own pupil or pupils to train, or keep doing solo missions.

"Room service for Mr. Devou," said the waitress to two of the guards.

"Come in, serve Mr. Devou, and leave," replied one guard. He watched her walk by and put thumbs up to the other guard who laughed.

The waitress set up the food, while Cullen poured the champagne making sure to leave poison only in the target's glass. As he and the waitress started leaving the room, the target hit the ground with a thump. At that moment Cullen started to run, but he couldn't leave the girl because she would be suspected too.

"Run!" shouted Cullen while grabbing the girl's hand. He could hear rifles being readied.

"Wait, why!?" replied the girl in fear.

"I'll tell you later, just stay here until I cover our escape," explained Cullen after they made it around the corner down the hall.

Cullen ran back down the hallway dodging bullets with his blur step, a disorienting short ranged teleportation. Whoever saw the teleportation became dizzy. By the time he made it to the end, the guards who stood in his way were dead thanks to Fang's razor-sharp curved blade. The six other guards to Cullen's left and right were bested by the same technique shortly after.

"Let's get out of here before the mistress calls for reinforcements," said Cullen with a kind smile, while holding out his hand.

"Why did you save me and why should I follow you!?" questioned the girl in a panic.

"I didn't want you to die for my mistake and if you don't follow me you *will* die," replied Cullen in a rushed voice.

A few minutes later the two made it out of the hotel and were out on the street a couple blocks away.

"Thanks for saving me," said the girl graciously and out of breath.

"I never should have gotten you involved in the first place," replied Cullen. He looked down with regret.

"True, now I can't possibly go back to working there," moped the girl. She held her head not knowing what to do.

"I'm so sorry, I'd be happy to give you half of my cut so you can survive until you find a new job."

"Wow, you're pretty nice for an Assassin," replied the girl while laughing.

"Could you please not tell anyone? Any infamy would make my job more dangerous."

"Sure, but on one condition."

"What would that be?"

"Give me your contact information."

"Why? Well, ok. I have to report in, so just contact me anytime tomorrow. Oh what was your name?" said Cullen, feeling a bit awkward and confused.

"I'm Sateer. What's yours or should I just call you Assassin?"

"I'm Cullen. See you," he replied with a puff into stealth for effect.

Chapter 2: New Prospects

"Your poison was too potent, Cullen. An alpha predator knows how to efficiently hunt. There's such a thing as overkill," lectured Fang.

"I found you when you were a pup, what could you possibly know about being an alpha predator?" wittily responded Cullen, as Fang jumped onto his bed bearing his teeth.

"You know I'm right, Cullen. I'm just trying to give you some advice because from now on it will just be you and me," growled Fang, as he started gnawing on Cullen's sleeve.

"You're right, when I mixed that poison all I had was the strong stuff. I figured that one drop would at least take five minutes to kick in," analyzed Cullen. He added to his personal alchemy notes.

The crowd gathered for the promotion ceremony where all trainees would become fully fledged Assassins. Everyone was lined up in anticipation to receive their mark to be placed on their wrist, as well as somewhere on both their weapon's forms. Fang wanted his on his hilt and left paw. When Cullen's turn came, he wasn't there.

"Cullen... Ahem... Ok... Next," said the announcer, who was joined by everyone in looking around.

"I'm here! Sorry I'm late," shouted Cullen, as he appeared out of thin air after touching the announcer on the shoulder. The crowd filled with laughter, while the Masters sitting up on the stage were frozen in astonishment. They did not sense his presence on his approach.

The trainee system is varied for the Assassins. A fully fledged Assassin starts at the age of 24, unless they show extraordinary talent. A full-fledged Assassin or just Assassin can do missions on their own, teach, or train 3 trainees at the same time. A Master Assassin can serve mandatory time on the council, take 1 trainee, or be a school teacher.

"You should take on 3 trainees, Cullen," suggested Fang, while sitting on Cullen's bed.

"I will definitely do that, but I want to find out where to live outside of Kelvar first," replied Cullen, while looking at a map of the universe.

"That's a good idea, we can go where ever we like! Someplace not too hot or cold and not too populated."

"Want to get out of the city Fang? Hmm... Let me find a place that fits that description," contemplated Cullen, as the phone started ringing.

"Hello? Ah Sateer, you actually called," joked Cullen.

"Of course I did. You couldn't tell that I liked you?" asked Sateer.

"Well, this kind of job doesn't provide many opportunities for fan girls. I'm mostly feared by everyone except for those within the order."

"I'm more than your average girl. I have a business proposition for you by the way. How would you like for me to be your pilot?"

"What's in it for you?"

"You can use my ship and my piloting skills for quick escapes and I can use your expertise to be my bodyguard, while smuggling my cargo."

"I'll consider your offer. I'd like to meet in person, so I can inspect your ship and get to know my business partner a little better," replied Cullen flirtatiously.

"Great, see you on Lexon at spaceport 2b," giggled Sateer as the call ended.

Spaceport 2b was plenty far away from the site of Cullen's last job, which provided a safe degree of anonymity. Sateer was waiting for him inside. They took a quick shuttle to where her ship was docked.

"Holy shit! This looks like a piece of junk! I don't think my interest is piqued at the moment," exclaimed Cullen.

"Just hold your tongue until we get inside," replied Sateer with a sigh as they walked up the ramp.

The ship was so clean and polished on the inside that it looked like a floor model. Everything seemed state of the art, but that was not the case to the trained eye.

"This was my father's ship, Hope's Arrow. I used up nearly all of my savings and the money you gave me to finish the customizations. Everything besides the ugly exterior consists of the best parts money can buy. It only looks ugly because this is a smuggling vessel."

"This ship looks wonderful!"

"Let's take her for a spin," said Fang with a smile, after changing into his animal form.

"Whoa, who's that?"

"I'm his dagger and best friend. I eat women like you for —" said Fang in a voice to frighten Sateer.

"He's so cute! I didn't know dogs could talk and transform!" replied Sateer as she petted Fang on the head.

"Hey! I'm a wolf! You —" grunted Fang, while his tail clearly wagged.

"Now now, Fang. At least she likes you," interrupted Cullen.

After all the introductions were through, Sateer flew them at first within the atmosphere and then up into space. She guaranteed warp speed, when it was necessary. Once the demonstration was over, the three of them sat down and planned their next step.

Cullen told her how he and Fang were looking for a new place to live, since they lived on Kelvar for most or all of their lives. Sateer said that the best way to find a new place to live was to scout it out for yourself. Taking her advice, Cullen decided to take in 3 trainees, while looking for his new place along the way. Sateer thought it was a great idea. As per her agreement with Cullen, she would be gaining three mini bodyguards.

"Bye puppy! See you soon!" teased Sateer, while sticking her tongue out and watching Fang transform back into a dagger.

"I'll call you when I've assembled my team," said Cullen in a professional manner, until his face turned red after Sateer gave him a peck on the cheek.

Chapter 3: My Own Team!?

"So I get to handpick the students I want from the various schools planet wide, right?" asked Cullen.

"Sorry, kiddo. I pick, but Assassins get assigned trainees by their teacher. If you were a Master like me, then you would have the ability to pick one or three students," replied Flint.

The children went to various academies around the Assassin's planet until the age of thirteen, when they received a master or went into another occupation. Other occupations included the Flight School, Teacher's College, Diviner's Circle, and the Research and Development College. All were just as important as the next.

"Oh, well when do I get to meet them?" asked Cullen who felt a little down, but still overall very excited.

"I already assembled them. Just head on over to the training field when you're ready. They're staying at the inn nearby to get to know each other. I'll call to let them know you're waiting," replied Flint.

"What do you think this guy is like?" asked Sera.

"His skill is all that really matters," answered Kai.

"I hope he's nice, he will be our teacher for a long time after all," added Cameron.

"Look, he isn't even here," stated Sera.

"Surprise! I'm happy to meet you all! I'm Cull —" shouted Cullen, as he showed up in an explosion similar to a flash of lightning.

"EEEYYYYAAAH!" screamed Cam as she ran away.

"HAH!" yelled Sera, as she instinctively punched Cullen so hard in the gut that he got the wind knocked out of him.

Kai just stood there for a few seconds with his arms crossed looking like he wasn't fazed at all, until he fell straight back after fainting.

"Are you crazy? I've never been surprised that much in my life!" yelled Kai.

"Sorry, I just wanted a memorable first impression for our team," explained Cullen.

"Are you okay, Cullen, I just reacted. I didn't mean to hurt you," said Sera, bowing apologetically.

"My teacher is a scary man!" cried Cam.

"I'm sorry. I'm treating you guys to lunch and you can order whatever you want," consoled Cullen.

"Wow, you're nice after all!" replied Cam.

"I saved your seats Cullen. I'd like to introduce your trainees' weapons, Slimy, Crawly, and Floaty," smiled Fang.

"Shut up, Fluffy!" replied the three weapons, a garden snake, a cobalt blue tarantula, and a golden finch.

"This whole ordeal was about first impressions, Fang," Cullen said with a sigh.

"What are you talking about? These kids worship me. Isn't that right, kids?" replied Fang, while the weapons quickly shook their heads.

"He's too into lecturing," pointed out the bird.

"True, but remember that he means well, despite his delivery. Anyway, since I already know my trainees, I'd like them to introduce their weapons and where they met them," said Cullen as he gestured to Sera.

Animals became tamed very early on. When children reached the age of 7 they would set out to tame an animal. Each taming was unique as it required a special encounter to foster a strong bond. The stronger children would journey deep into the wilderness, while weaker ones simply went out into their backyard. Two variables that made a difference include quality and the strength of the initial bond. Finding a rare species definitely didn't hurt. Ideally, an Assassin and a weapon should be the best of friends.

"I was deep in the rainforest searching for the perfect weapon, when suddenly I felt something drop onto my head. I picked it up and it turned out to be a huge tarantula, which didn't change my mind about wanting to throw it as far as possible. Then, he said..." queuing her weapon to finish the story.

"Please don't throw me! I accidentally fell off a tree leaf after a monkey passed by!" finished the spider.

"And Jeff and I have been best friends ever since," said Sera, as Jeff lovingly crawled onto her shoulder.

"I'll go next, I suppose. Cheri over here saved my life from a terrible disease!" explained Kai, as everyone around the table looked at each other in confusion.

"Let me tell it Kai, you're just going to make it sound weird. This kid was sitting on his front porch near the dorm garden reading a book, when he started freaking out over this mouse I was stalking. I snatched it up and attempted to slither on out of there, but he kept thanking me," explained Cheri.

"I could've died from the plague!" exclaimed Kai, as he shuddered and put on some hand sanitizer.

"Well, I'm all that's left. I bought Akiko at a pet shop," plainly said Cam.

"Why would you do that, don't the best weapons come from the wild?" asked Cullen.

"My reason was genius. You see all animals are inherently wild, but most don't even want to become weapons. Pets, on the other hand, don't get a choice as to what they get to be," started Cam. She got more into it by gesturing with her hands. "I decided to find an animal doomed to be a pet who truly desired to become a weapon. When I heard Akiko in the corner looking so sad, I knew I could do my best to give her the life of a weapon." She was filled with nostalgia.

"And in return, I make sure she doesn't get caught up in her inventions too much," added Akiko.

"Cullen, since we're on the subject, how did you meet Fang over here?" asked Sera out of curiosity.

"I was deep in the Forgotten Forest when I suddenly collapsed from exhaustion. I had been there for a week searching for a wolf that would join me, but every time I found one, they ran off. The other forest animals all laughed at me for trying to tame a wolf, but I never gave up. I passed out from lack of food and exhaustion. When I came to, I was surrounded by a whole pack. The alpha told me that he would grant me a cub from his pack if I could hold my own against his father. They didn't even let me use a weapon. Anyways, I managed to not die, which was more than can be said for the candidates before me. The alpha told me that he would be happy to grant me Fang because he only allowed me the chance due to my strength and determination against the odds. He told me that the reason for the challenge was so that access to their kind wouldn't end up diminishing their prestige," told Cullen, with his trainees' eyes filled with wonderment.

"It was an honor for me to serve him, especially since so many before him had failed," added Fang in a serious tone.

"I hear the Grand Master's weapon is from that village," stated Sera.

"My great grandmother," said Fang.

"Wow you're like royalty, Fang!" said Akiko with praise.

"Our stories are pitiful compared to yours, Cullen," admitted Kai sadly.

"The bond between our weapons is the most important part. For example, if I was saved by Fang before he became my weapon, we would never mesh as a team because I don't need someone to save me," explained Cullen.

"He needs someone who shares his ambition and cunning," added Fang.

"It seems like it's different for each pair, since me and Sera bonded through compassion and understanding," analyzed Jeff.

"Kai needed me to watch his back and not much has changed," stated Cheri.

"Cam saved me from winding up as some old ladies tweety bird, so the least I can do is keeping her in check. A mutual partnership in my opinion."

"This has been good, you guys. Understanding the bonds between you and your weapons will allow you to unlock new abilities," explained Cullen waiting for an excited response.

"They didn't teach us that at school. What kind are we talking about here?" questioned Sera.

"It all depends on three things, your primary and secondary skills, your weapon's animal traits, and the situation that creates the urgency for said skill."

"This is so cool! Tell us more, Cullen!" said Cam and Akiko.

"What kind of ability do you have, Cullen?" asked Kai.

"You'll see it one day, if we ever get in a big enough pinch," said Cullen as he was drowned out in a sea of disappointed noises.

"Thanks for the food Cullen. I haven't been here before," said Kai in appreciation.

"Ok, now that lunch is over, I want you guys to prepare for a little test over on top that hill at 5 o'clock," ordered Cullen in a serious voice, as his trainees nodded and got up to leave.

When the three kids showed up, Cullen was listening to music through headphones and Fang seemed to show indirect enjoyment as he lay on the grass. Cullen waved them over and gestured for them to walk over to a nearby hill with nothing but grass. This was so that there wouldn't be anywhere to hide unless one could activate stealth.

"I want all of you to try to knock me on my back using non-lethal means. By non-lethal, I mean your weapons need to be dull and poisons and traps can only temporarily knock someone out. The first one to do so is dismissed from the fight, the same goes for the second. The person that is left has five minutes to complete the task. Any questions? Ok, begin!"

Cullen pulled out his dagger into a defensive stance with the blade facing his elbow as he assessed the situation. Kai summoned his katana, readying a draw stance. It was a bold move to even consider ending his engagement with the first strike. Kai's strike flew at incredible speed, but Cullen punished him for his foolishness by blur stepping out of the way, leaving the boy swinging at air. A confident smile appeared on Kai's face as he witnessed Cullen getting blown off his feet, from the gust of wind generated by the lesser wind potion that coated Kai's blade. Cullen would have hit his face flat on the ground, if he didn't spring himself back up with his hands.

Taking full advantage of the opportunity was non-other than Sera with her double chain scythe. Seeing her when she activated her stealth gave Cullen the foresight to expect a sneak attack. He grabbed her leg after twisting mid-air to send her flying. Now, Kai came back at Cullen with an onslaught of desperate slashes of wind that flew from each swing. This forced not only Cullen to maneuver out of the way of these flying obstacles, but everyone else as well.

After Kai obviously couldn't produce anymore wind, he and Sera rushed Cullen from both sides. Just when they both were about to attack, Cam saw her opportunity to win. Using all the strength she could muster, she threw her halberd like a boomerang at all three of them. Taken completely off guard the three of them were blasted off the hill, rolling all the way down.

"Yay! We're first!" cheered Akiko and Cam, with Akiko in bird form again.

A couple minutes later the three victims made it back up the hill, ready to resume. Kai and Sera decided to cut their losses and flip a coin to see who would get to fight one on one with Cullen. They didn't care what place they finished in as long as the end result was Cullen being knocked down by both of them.

Sera sprinted right at Cullen and threw one scythe that was deflected into the air. After jumping over him, she pulled the airborne scythe down, while striking with the one still in her hand. Sera scratched Cullen's arm, which soon after became numb. Now that he had a major handicap she threw some attacks to tie him up, until she finally wrapped her chain around Cullen's foot tossing him as far as she could. He hit the ground with a flop.

"Now it's my turn to finally get you, Cullen," declared Kai in anger and frustration.

"Throwing down the gauntlet are we?" replied Cullen with a dead serious face.

Cullen made the first move by switching to an offensive stance by pointing his dagger at Kai and turning to the side in preparation for a lunge. Seeing this as a challenge, Kai went back to his draw stance. They both waited for any kind of movement. Once they felt that twitch signaling the proper time to strike, they made their move. Even though they began at the same time, Cullen's dagger was at Kai's throat by the time he even touched the hilt of his katana. Feeling defeated, Kai gave up. Cullen had to make an example of someone.

"Now, I need to explain some things to you guys. You all made mistakes and successes, both big and small. I decided to let you pass or fail this exercise depending on your overall performance. Firstly, I let Cam win because she waited for the right time to strike, so much so that Kai and Sera didn't see it coming. I thought if Kai and Sera were going to get hit, then I should as well in order to fool Cam.

Then, I gave Sera a fair second chance to up her game after the coin toss. I let her pass because instead of hastily taking the easy win, she opted to weaken me with a numbing poison. Kai had very impressive swordsmanship. Unfortunately he grew frustrated, leading to potential collateral damage if it were a real world situation. I really had to show Kai some humility, because he was too eager for revenge when it came down to his last chance.

Sera came across as a bit hasty from her first attack, but I cut her some slack since it might have worked on a non-stealth expert. Cam did a great job with her attack, but she stood there like a log," lectured Cullen. Sera took every bit of criticism to heart. Kai's pride was wounded, yet Cheri hissed in his ear causing his mood to look more appreciative. Cam was crying and taking notes at the same time.

"That was a priceless experience," commented Sera as she wiped the perspiration from her forehead.

"I need to control my emotions," reflected Kai hanging his head.

"I'll be perfect next time!" announced Cam with a clenched fist.

"I'm proud of you guys! Take a couple days to pack for a long trip. Be ready to meet me at the city's spaceport when I call."

Chapter 4: The Date

"Sateer, is that a basket and water/food bowl? I am not a dog!" barked Fang, once they got back onto her ship.

"Oh, does that mean you don't want it? I'll just return it then," acted Sateer seeing full well the twinkle in his eyes.

"Don't be ridiculous, since you went through the trouble of setting it up, it would be a waste to return it now," hastily replied Fang, as he fluffed the pillow and moved the bowl to a more desirable position.

"Is this your wife, Cullen? She fine, ack!" said Kai as Cheri choked him in order to get him to realize his rudeness.

"I just met her recently. She's just my business partner," answered Cullen.

"He saved my life, I asked for HIS contact information, we became business partners, AND I tried to make it more obvious that I like him by kissing him on the cheek. Guess what?" polled Sateer.

"Still hasn't asked you out!? Cullen, that's terrible," said Cam, while wagging her finger.

"It sounds like the odds are in your favor," added Jeff, as he crawled out of Sera's pocket.

"Fine, dinner tomorrow night?" asked Cullen.

"I accept. Girls, can you help Cullen pick out something nice to wear? We're going to a snazzy restaurant," said Sateer.

The girls started going through Cullen's wardrobe out of what he had with him and it didn't look very promising. He has never wanted to stand out in public before. Everything about his physical appearance could be made to look average even though he was a handsome enough guy. He had medium long black hair with some grey in it even though it betrayed his youth. He stood at about five-seven with a medium physique. His complexion was on the tanner side. It was decided that the girls needed to take him to the market and grab him a nice enough outfit.

"I'm not going in this penguin suit," blatantly stated Cullen.

"It looks great! Right, Sera?" replied Cam.

"You'll wear it if you like her. I think you two would make a good couple. Do your best, Cullen!" replied Sera, while motivating her Master.

"If she'll like it, then I'll bear with it," replied Cullen with a sigh.

"On top of fashion tips, Cam and I are going to give you advice on what to do during your date," added Sera, carrying a hush-hush attitude.

"Here, before you meet her put this in your ear," said Cam, as she handed him the tiny communication device.

"Kai, we're going to sneak into the restaurant and spy on their date. I don't want you in your room, while everyone else is having fun," ordered Cheri.

"We're all going too," said Fang, as he waltzed into the room.

"How did you get in here?" asked Kai.

"Shut up," replied Fang.

"Yeah, you think us weapons are just going to be on standby?" added Jeff, while crawling on the ceiling.

"I'm rooting for my girl's fashion sense here!" said Akiko on a side note.

"Hey, are you hungry?" asked Cullen as he greeted Sateer.

"WHAT WAS THAT? WE JUST GAVE YOU YOUR LINES!" shouted both the girls, just before Cullen pulled out his communication device, crushed it, and threw it in an inconspicuous manner, of course.

"I'm starving, I barely ate anything all day," replied Sateer as they started towards the entrance to the restaurant, Zaorko's Finest.

"How dare he destroy my communication device? Those don't come cheap, you know?" said Sera.

"We were only trying to help," sobbed Cam, as she blew her nose.

"Wanna go spy on them?" asked Sera, in an attempt to console Cam.

"Yeah," Cam sniveled, as she started to calm down a bit.

"I have no idea what to order. I've never had enough money to go to one of these places," stated Sateer.

"I would go for anything containing a meat that you have already had. Stay away from exotic sounding creatures," replied Cullen.

"So you don't know what to order either?"

"Yeah, but I've been all across the universe and I've learned how to make a safe bet."

"So do you enjoy all the traveling?"

"I love it, but I've never had a place I really belong to. I've always felt like a spectator in my own life. I guess that's why I want to find a nice home now that I can move off of the Assassin's planet."

"Well what about your family? Where were you born?"

"I was given to the Assassins as a newborn. I know my parents, but my home has always been with the Assassins."

Each Assassin was not born on the planet Kelvar. They were chosen to serve by those called the Diviners. They examined newborns from each planet. Newborns got their blood drawn. Those samples would be reviewed by the Diviners, who meditated over large shipments. No kind of spine tingling ritual took place. It just made the process go by more quickly. Certain vials resonated more strongly than others within the minds of the Diviners. This information alone decided who would be trained as an Assassin. This process practiced ever since the beginning of the Assassins produced excellent results. As long as no Assassin's progeny made the cut, all the selected vials would be used.

From there the Assassins would personally visit the families and propose the training. The families were under no obligation to accept, but there were certain perks to agreeing. Their children would receive a top notch education, room and boarding, and would one day make a lot of money that could be used to support them when they grew old. The Assassins also maintained a lofty prestige as being the great balance of power in the universe. Having a son or daughter as an Assassin brought immeasurable honor to one's family.

"I see, I've always lived here, but I still don't feel like this is my home. Now I can travel around the universe like you!"

"Don't go without my protection, it's a nasty place. I don't want to see you hurt."

"How sweet! I didn't know you Assassins had a heart."

"True there are some who lose their soul to the pleasure of killing, but I try to find the true purpose of my trade. Sometimes I don't even fully understand what the reason for its existence is. Maybe that's just because they've been an institution for so long."

"Cullen's so getting some. That's my partner for you. His heart always draws people in," stated Fang, while sheathed on Kai's belt.

"He's smooth, when he's not trying so hard. You should learn from him, Kai," observed Cheri as she whispered into Kai's ear.

"Taking mental notes as we speak. You think I have a chance with Sera?" replied Kai.

"You would need to impress her with your skill. That's the impression that I get from her. I could ask Cam what she thinks about you, if you want," advised Akiko, without forgetting to advertise her beloved partner.

"Is it okay if I try to catch that fly over there?" asked Jeff.

"You're gonna scare off the customers!" replied Kai.

"Fine, but you owe me some bugs later, here's a reminder," replied Jeff in an irritated mood. He spun some web in Kai's hood where he and Akiko were hiding.

"Hey, Kai, over here!" whispered Sera from the hallway leading to the communication booth.

"So you guys are spying too? That's pretty hilarious," said Kai, while showing his occasional laugh.

"It's a long story," replied Sera with a sigh.

"Cullen's a meanie," pouted Cam.

"Sera, I'm starving. Is there cricket anything on the menu?" moped Jeff, as he crawled back onto his partner's shoulder.

"Let's go ask the kitchen. I don't want to get caught," replied Sera, as she and Jeff walked off.

"Cam, what do you think of —" started Akiko, while jumping out of Kai's hood and onto his head.

"Not now!" whispered Kai, before Akiko could embarrass him.

"Do you like Sera?" asked Cam.

"NO! Where did you get a crazy idea like that?" instantly replied Kai, showing some extreme nervousness.

"Want some help?"

"See we're here for you, Kai," smiled Akiko.

"It's a good offer, you should take it," advised Cheri.

"Don't listen to these ladies kid. Come under the tutelage of the Alpha Predator in the room. She'll love you for life. Remember that wolves mate for life," proposed Fang.

"This better work, Fang. This is all completely out of my comfort zone. I'm getting nervous just thinking about it," said Kai as he bravely accepted.

"Don't eat too fast Jeff. Save some for later too. Can you guys believe we haven't been caught yet?" declared Sera.

"That's because they're gone," answered Fang as he walked back into the hallway.

"So, how did it go last night?" asked Cam.

"The meal was great and so was everything else, but then Cullen passed out and I had to take him back to my room at the ship. He was out cold. I tried to wake him and checked if he had some sort of sickness, but he just seemed tired," explained Sateer.

"I woke up in her bed," muttered Cullen still feeling groggy.

"Why didn't you just leave him in one of the guest rooms?" asked Cam.

"Well, he did such a good job on our date that I thought he deserved a reward. We didn't do anything. Just slept," explained Sateer in all honesty.

"Rape!" exclaimed Kai.

"It's not rape if you want it," added Fang.

"Oh come on guys! What they do during their private time is none of our business, no matter how juicy," giggled Sera.

"Honey, I love how you don't snore," said Sateer as she wrapped her arms around Cullen.

"Training," he replied, while clearly enjoying the affection.

"You guys are too much! Can we get some breakfast?" asked Jeff.

"I want you guys to pick your rooms and unpack your things today. My old room is available, since I'll be moving into Sateer's room," ordered Cullen.

"That was fast," whispered Kai to his teammates.

"Life's too short Kai. You should know that by know," said Cullen, as he winked and looked at Sera.

Sera really was a beauty too, with her long straight white hair, almost like snow. She was quite skinny, which made sense since she was only thirteen. She stood a little taller than Kai, who had good fit muscles for his age. He had medium long blond hair that went down to his neck in the back and long bangs in the front. Cam immediately started running towards one of the rooms with her sky blue hair shining in the light. It was on the wavy side at about half of the length of Sera's hair making it just above her shoulders. She was a little more physically matured than Sera, though all three teammates were thirteen. Sateer was truly someone the girls could look up to in terms of beauty. She sported long pink hair that matched perfectly with her yellow, almost catlike eyes. Her womanly features were typical of someone who took good care of themselves in their health. Her fair complexion was typical of her race, which came from the casino planet Cullen had found her on.

Everyone was unpacked by the end of the day. They had brought all the necessary supplies for a long trip, long being an unknown amount of time. Their rooms had a few personal decorations, because they learned at the academy that it helps to feel at home where ever you are. Sera filled her room with all sorts of books. Some were for fun, but also a good deal of reference manuals for the field. Digital books were available, but she grew attached to her printed books and liked to take special notes in them. Her most prized possession always sitting on her bed was a stuffed monkey, which she can't sleep without. Kai's room had a poster of his favorite swordsman, the Sorrowful Hunter. He enjoyed dim lighting in his room for meditation so he had a lamp that emanated a dark red light. Cam had all of her different outfits hanging on the wall, already assembled. She liked to be able to see them collectively and make adjustments. She also had a fantasy poster she drew of the kind of Master Assassin she aspired to be when she grew up, to help keep her motivated. Cullen only had two personal effects in his and Sateer's room, a seven day prayer pamphlet and crest that he wears whenever he goes out. Everything else included the clothes he put in the drawers Sateer cleared for him. The weapons were free to set up their living quarters where ever they wanted around the ship. They were also welcome to stay with their respective partners.

"Okay, so all of my cargo consists of either food or medicine that is relatively easy for us to get, but hard for others in certain planets across the universe. I'm only working with you guys and Cullen, so I'm basing our destinations on rumors," explained Sateer.

"Fang and I asked around the spaceport bars and shops. We heard that there is a planet that lies on the border of the Venhinge Empire and uncontrolled territory. The planet in question is called Formota," added Cullen.

"The wilderness planet full of mining camps set up by the Empire. I heard the residents are forced to work for little pay. However, the military presence is light. It should be easy for us to move freely," explained Sera, feeling very proud of herself.

"There's an ancient relic there. No one's ever found it," added Kai.

"Don't even think about it! You know how dangerous relic trials are," snapped Cheri, as she squeezed his neck.

"I have a relic and it was no picnic Kai. I'm only here today because the relic decided to revive me," warned Cullen.

"Back to the mission! You trainees will covertly escort Sateer while she's making the delivery. Cullen and I will head to the destination ahead of you to make sure there isn't any foul play. The most important thing to remember is that you cannot kill anyone. We don't want a Death Mark on Sateer. Also, you all need to wear masks with this symbol. I have four colors, red, yellow, blue, and black. Pick whichever you like. We just don't want our personal lives mixing with our jobs," explained Fang, as he finished the briefing.

Formota was one giant mountainous region filled with forests and rivers. Deep in the mountains were precious stones and metals used for jewelry or technological devices. The people didn't get a bit of profit, but the Venhinge Empire sure did. In each region existed large mines, but due to the rough terrain and vicious beasts there were only a few scattered settlements. Ixue was hit especially hard by the mining operations, but were hung out to dry when the resources were depleted due to over mining. They were left to their own devices without any help from their Empire who went on to other regions of Formota.

Sateer dropped Cullen and Fang off in the forest about 20 miles from the city of Ixue. Once he gave the go ahead the rest of the group would land in the city's spaceport to drop off the food and medicine.

"There are an awfully large amount of dangerous predators around here," stated Fang, already on his guard.

"Better transform."

"Right."

The two of them carefully trekked toward the city. The two counted as least three major predators, making the giant wall surrounding the city a necessity. Since Cullen could mask his presence he did not have any major encounters. Fang tried going off on his own a couple times to talk to some local animals to ask why there was such tension in this area. They said the people in the city have been dying from sickness and starvation causing an imbalance in the region. The smell of death and desperation is driving the animals angry and afraid. The different animals are becoming more territorial and aggressive towards each other. Fang told them not to worry and to not attack his friends. A little while later they reached the front gate.

"Who goes there?" asked the gatekeeper.

"I represent Sateer," replied Cullen.

"Let me check the list. One moment please."

"This man looks frail, Cullen," said Fang.

"We'll help this city get back on their feet."

"You check out. Please come in and head straight to the mayor's office," announced the gatekeeper.

Fang and Cullen were guided to the mayor's office. All along the way, citizens were heading to the doctor to check if their medicine was ready. It was not. The hungry begged for food, but the shopkeepers were rationing for themselves just to keep the business running at the very least.

"Are you Sateer's business partner? I'm Mayor Tergen, it's a pleasure and a blessing to meet you," said the Mayor, as he shook Cullen's hand.

"Hi, I'm Night. Are you ready to receive the delivery?" answered Cullen, who used the name Night because he dawned a black mask and wanted to hide his identity.

"Yes, we are in dire need of these supplies, but the payment might be hard for us to come by at this time."

"Oh, please don't worry about the money until you're back on your feet Mr. Mayor. I couldn't take advantage of a suffering city.

Just give me an hour to check your city. This is just a security precaution for my employees, I assure you,"

"Of course take your time Night."

Fang and Cullen began their check immediately. Everything seemed normal. This town really was abandoned by its government. This conclusion brought a bitter sweet taste to Fang and Cullen's mouths.

"Sateer, you guys can land at the spaceport. You're clearance code is 401B8L," said Cullen over the communicator.

"Got it, see you there."

The three students walked out of the ship, while pushing carts of supplies. Kai wore the red mask, Sera's was blue, and Cam's was yellow, her favorite color. Sateer walked out pushing a cart as well, until she saw the mayor and Cullen walking towards the ship.

"Thank you for your charity, Sateer. We will never forget," said the mayor, as he shook her hand and began to cry.

"Of course, I'm sure the money will come before we know it," she replied with a smile.

"About the money, I have a proposition of a form of payment that will make you infinitely more money."

"I'm listening."

"Rago, come here. I'd like you to meet Rago, a fine hunter and pilot."

"You're dumping your kid on me?"

"Of course not. I love my son. It's just that he has always dreamed of getting off this planet and being a great pilot for the Empire, but he got kicked out of the academy for fighting with one of his instructors about the ideologies the school promoted. What was it son?"

"Kill with no remorse. You are a weapon of destruction. Your Emperor is your conscience," regurgitated Rago.

"I like you already, welcome aboard Hope's Arrow. You can be my co-pilot, but I'll let you fly by yourself. If you like," said Sateer as she gave him a welcome hug.

"We're going to stay here a week or so to unload and help redistribute the goods," explained Cullen.

"Sounds good. So what do we tell the new guy?" asked Kai.

"He's part of the crew, we tell him everything, and if he blabs then we know who to kill first."

"Okay. Can me, Rago, and the girls explore the wilderness and train a little for a day?"

"Sure. Just be back before the next sunrise."

"Hey, Rago, are there any legends about some sort of mysterious cave or forbidden place in the wilderness in this region?" asked Kai.

"Yeah, there's Mt. Shreako. It's a famous legend in Ixue. Long ago before Ixue even existed there was a young hunter who came through this region in order to complete his hometowns map of the surrounding areas. He had a kind and courageous heart, which fostered great respect from the animals of the wilderness. It was said that he only killed in order to satisfy his most basic needs for food and in turn received an ever peaceful passage through the wilderness. It was then that the wise and powerful mountain spirit named Ix invited the young hunter into his mountain and dwelling to reward his kind soul. Ix warned the hunter that once he entered he could not come out until he successfully passed the ascending labyrinth leading to the peak of the mountain. Of course the courageous hunter accepted the invitation. Many hours later the hunter emerged from within the mountain's peak having faced the perilous and daunting trials. The power he gained was such that he himself created the grand city of Ixue in honor of the wise spirit Ix," replied Rago.

"Best campfire story ever," announced Jeff.

"Forget about what I said earlier, you're getting that relic Kai" added Cheri.

"You can't! I just met you! We're all such good friends now! I don't want you to die!" shouted Cam all in a fit.

"Try drawing a map like the young hunter in the story," advised Sera.

"Does no one else think this is a terrible idea?!" shouted Cam.

"I don't want to disagree with you, but you need to be brave in our line of work," Akiko sighed.

"Well, we better get going. This way, it's not that far," said Rago, as he put out the fire.

"Remember in order to gain the relic's power you have to go in alone, with no weapon," explained Sera, as she gave him a good luck hug with Cam coming over afterward.

"Your training and bravery will get you through. Also the qualities of the young hunter were a kind soul and bravery," advised Cam, while she hugged him as well.

"Okay, here I go. A kind heart and a brave soul," said Kai, repeating the former as he walked pass the warning signs on the walls of the entrance.

Once Kai crossed the threshold, his surroundings completely changed.

"Welcome young one. This is my home. Many perilous trials await you that will test your mind, body, and soul. Make it through the ascending labyrinth and out to the mountain's peak at the top and gain great power. Good luck. I pray for your success," announced the wise spirit Ix, with a voice sounding like a woman in her mid-twenties or thirties.

Kai started down the path and he immediately saw animals of all sorts, but it did not seem like they were in physical form. They seemed like spirits of animals dead and gone. Some saw him and bore their fangs showing aggression. Kai put his guard up, feeling discouraged without his weapon. The tigers lunged at him and he attempted to fight back. He was badly injured by the onslaught, although he won. Suddenly something strange happened and baby tigers rushed to the side of the fallen and began bearing their fangs. Kai felt remorse for he had killed their mother or next to kin. He lowered his guard and bowed his head asking for forgiveness. The young cubs bowed back, grew into adulthood, and walked to his side. He could hear them as if they were a weapon like Cheri.

"You have passed the test of kindness for you have shown remorse for your mistakes. We three are now your allies and will obey your commands as long as you do not forget what you have learned this day. I am Rai, he is Sui, and she is Fuu," said Rai, the eldest brother of the three Bengal Tigers.

"Would you happen to know the way through this labyrinth?"

"We can take you as far as the trial of courage about half way up."

"Thank you so much. Shall we?"

About two hours later the four made it half way up the mountain. Kai realized that his new friends were similar to a go between for the communicating with the other animal spirits. As long as he was with them he faced no danger from other animals, even the especially scary ones.

"We're here. Unfortunately we cannot help you at this stage. If you pass the test of courage, we will rendezvous with you on the next floor. Good luck Kai," explained Rai before he and his siblings vanished.

Kai walked this time down the bridged path over a lava pit keeping courage in his heart. Strangely it seemed peaceful enough and he could see the entrance. He started walking a little further when suddenly he heard a voice over at an intersection of the bridge to the left.

"Please, I know I stole from your territory, but I have nowhere else to go. Just let me go and you'll never see me again," cried a tiny snapping turtle.

"I don't care! You know the rules of the forest. If you want something, then you have to trade," hollered a giant gorilla.

"I have nothing to give, I can return when I find something valuable," pleaded the turtle.

"How about I have myself some turtle soup!" replied the gorilla, as he began to lift his arm to smash the turtle.

"Wait!" shouted Kai as he rushed over to save the turtle.

"Huh? What do you want?" asked the gorilla in disgust.

"Here I have a, let me see. How about a piece of paper and pencil?" asked Kai?

"That pencil is too tiny for my hand. I'd break it in two seconds. I'll break you in two seconds if you don't get out of here!" replied the gorilla.

"I won't leave until you give the turtle a chance," replied Kai.

"Ha, I guess I'll just have to kill the both of you! HWAAA!!" yelled the gorilla as he pounded his fists and charged at Kai.

Kai really started to regret attempting to save a stupid little turtle instead of moving on, until the turtle that had already walked over to the gorillas feet chomped on his toe. Crying due to the excruciating pain, the gorilla tried to shake off the turtle, but he would not let go. Kai saw this as an opportunity to move in for the kill. He ran up to the gorilla and kicked the gorilla square in the chest with all his might, while yelling for the turtle to let go. The gorilla flew only about three feet, but just enough to send him off the walkway into a lava pit.

"Thanks for saving me from that brute. You showed not courage for yourself, but the courage to protect the weak. I may not look like much now, but check this out," said the snapping turtle, who transformed into a turtle shell shield.

"Whoa, you're an amazing shield, so light too!" replied Kai in amazement.

"That's right. And since I'm a snapping turtle anyone who attacks this shield receives a painful bite on their body, even from afar," explained Shelly.

"I'm glad I saved you now," laughed Kai.

"Let's get you to the mountain's peak."

A couple more hours later Shelly, Kai, and the Tiger Triplets made their way to the peak.

"So you did make it after all! You must be weary. Come here dear and have a meal with me," said Ix in a welcoming voice.

"You are probably the most beautiful women I have ever seen in my life," replied Kai.

"Why thank you. The young hunter said the same thing! Ha-ha," laughed Ix.

"Did you know that Ix looks like the most beautiful women to any man because her form is based on each man's preferences?" asked Sui.

"How could I possibly know that?" replied Kai in astonishment.

"Kai! You made it!" screamed Cam, as she rushed over to greet him.

"Yeah, it wasn't what I expected at all, but that's what made it challenging," replied Kai.

"So, let's see it," added Sera.

"Okay. Ix!" said Kai as he activated his relic.

"COOL!" clamored all.

"Are they weapons or what," questioned Sera.

"Shelly over here is a..." started Kai.

"Counter attacking shield," finished Shelly.

"And Sui, Rai, and Fuu..." started Kai.

"Can influence people and animals," finished the Tiger Triplets.

"Oh, people too?" asked Kai.

"Yeah, but the command only lasts for five minutes, then they wake up and wonder where they are. It's quite hilarious, really," explained Fuu.

"Don't say that, he's a kid who might abuse it!" said Rai.

"Sorry," replied Fuu.

"This is so close to home for me. You're like a reincarnation of my city's most famous legend! I'm so glad I joined your group," clamored Rago.

"You're growing on us too, young hunter. Man, I love that story. Let's get some breakfast back in town, it's almost sunrise," declared Jeff.

"Looks like someone, went out and got their relic anyways, huh?" smiled Cullen.

"HOW THE HELL DO YOU KNOW!" yelled all.

"You're not ready to know," replied Cullen.

"Did you follow us?" asked Sera.

"What are you talking about? He was here with me the whole time," added Sateer.

"Believe me I can vouch for that. Seriously did you guys sleep at —" started Fang.

"Hey, come on man. Not in front of the kids!" spouted Cullen.

"Oh my! Gah!" giggled Kai until Cheri squeezed his neck for being immature.

"Anyway, it looks like we're done here. What do you say we get off this planet and drop you guys back off at the Assassin's planet?" announced Sateer.

"Can I fly?" asked Rago timidly.

"Of course you can. I said so didn't I? My little co-pilot," lovingly replied Sateer.

"No, it's young hunter," giggled the kids.

"Sounds like you've got yourself a codename, unless you want people knowing your Venhingean," joked Cullen.

"Of course not. And it's Formotan only!" replied Rago sternly.

"Wait, aren't we smuggling a kid out of the Venhingean Empire?" asked Sera.

"So? What's the problem," asked Cullen.

"Isn't it illegal?" replied Sera.

"Not if your business is helping people," added Sateer.

Chapter 6: A Big Decision

"Man, we've been with Cullen for three years already. Can you believe it?" asked Cam.

"Yes. Time doesn't go by as fast as you think," replied Kai.

"True. The three of us have been working hard to get where we are today. I mean we're lucky to still be alive and healthy," noted Sera.

"Yeah a lot of my friends didn't make it this far and others are too injured to do any field work," sighed Kai.

"Hello? Okay see you there," said Sera into her communicator.

"Mission time?" asked Kai.

"Not that kind," replied Sera.

"Yes!" cheered Cam.

"Today we're helping Ixue and its revolutionary army takes back the last Imperial stronghold on Formota," explained Sateer.

"That whole smuggling thing didn't last very long, did it?" concluded Kai.

"It was pretty obvious that Cullen and I wanted more than to run a charity, right?"

"Very, at least it was once Ixue 'decided' to break from their terrible government."

"Right, but we need to also make sure that the planet doesn't get swallowed up by the Fulmer Empire either."

"How did we do this without killing anyone?"

"Because I'm such a good teacher!" said Cullen with a smile as he puffed into the picture.

"I can't believe we watched the whole thing from our ship. How boring," said Fang with a sigh.

"The citizens of Zexue were well prepared once their fellow Formotans arrived. It seems the Empire has given up," added Sera.

"It looks like we've won Sateer, thanks for... Wait this can't be. A decent amount of our own troops have turned and started attacking their comrades!" announced the now General Tergen of Ixue over the communicator.

"It's the Assassins, we need to get down there now!" ordered Cullen.

"Don't forget to wear your masks and your code names. Let's hear them. First Kai, Sera, and then Cam. Go," ordered Fang.

"Crimson."

"Rain."

"Light."

"Be careful guys," replied Sateer.

"This is too dangerous. If they try to kill you, use deadly force," ordered Cullen.

"The code," replied Sera.

"We're saving lives here! You know that right? What have I been teaching you these past few years? Why do you think you three are some of the best who came out of the academy? How many of your old classmates have fallen and for what? Look what we have built in the past few years! Can you honestly turn your back on that?" lectured Cullen, in one of his shining moments as a mentor.

The three sixteen year olds knew that their lives as Assassins were over. Their home since childhood will never let them go until they die or worse. They knew what they had to do and it was terrifying, but they trusted their mentor. Cullen never betrayed his friends and they trusted him with their lives.

"Open the hatch already!" shouted Kai.

"You ready, Jeff?" asked Sera.

"Our path is with you, Cullen," nodded Cam.

"Lower the ship dear and stay at a safe distance. Watch after her. Okay, Rago?" said Cullen, as he gave them possibly his last order.

"I didn't expect to see you here, Master Flint" said Cullen in a stern voice.

"You finally did it."

"Wait, what?"

"You found your own path."

"I don't understand. Why aren't you attacking me?"

"The code is bull, am I right?"

"Ha, you can say that again."

"I knew I could never acquire the power to bring down the Assassins, so I did the best I could in training you."

"You know I wasn't the best at the academy. I was the quiet one in class. I always felt left out. My best friend abandoned me and you were the only one who understood me."

"That's because you were never meant to be an Assassin no matter how good you are at it now."

"You always followed your heart and did what you thought was right. I let you foster that and look at you now. So here's what I'm going to do. You 'defeat' me and help your team. Find somewhere we can't find you. When the time comes, I'll be there for you as an agent on the inside. We can do this. Let's carve a path for a better future and bring some sense into our accursed existence and murderers."

"Thank you Master Flint. Wait for me until then. Don't drink so much! So shall we end this standoff in style?"

"You know me too well."

In a flash, Cullen fake slew his Master and went off to help his students, wherever they were.

"Please don't do this. I don't want to hurt you. Just go home," pleaded Kai to a fellow Assassin.

"You know I can't do that. I can't kill you either because of the code. Just surrender and you may only get a minor punishment," answered the Assassin.

"Awe, screw you man. I was trying to be nice! Sah!" yelled Kai as he slaughtered his first Assassin.

"Damn it! You'll never get away with this as long as you live!" said the Assassin in his dying screams.

Cutting through one Assassin's Achilles' tendon and through another's thigh muscle, Sera couldn't bear directly killing Assassins. If they died later, at least she didn't have to see it. It still killed her insides, but she new in her heart that she was doing this to save an entire planet.

Cam was completely absorbed by her just cause to the point of blindly following Cullen's orders. She was out to kill. She threw her Halberd with such ferocity at the enemy that it flew through multiple Assassins at one time. She almost didn't know who she was anymore because she only felt rage at the Assassins who she used to belong to.

"Cam! Stop it! This is too much! You could knock them out if you wanted to and you know that!" yelled Akiko, trying to wake up Cam from her trance.

"They were going to undue all the good we've done for these people."

"I know, but this is not the way. Cam! CAM! Mass Healing!" Akiko shouted with all of her might, bringing out something within.

Something welled up inside Akiko and surrounded Cam which then shot out towards all of those harmed by Akiko. They suddenly got up, were healed of their wounds, and fell into a peaceful slumber.

"Cam there you are, let's get out of here," said Cullen, who arrived right after she snapped out of it.

"Huh? Oh, right," replied Cam.

"There's too many of them!" said Sera feeling out of breath.

"It looks like they have a healer with them," added Jeff.

"What do we do Jeff?"

"I got this. Oh great spider, bestow onto me the strength to protect my friend from eminent danger. I'm willingly ready to sacrifice my life for hers. I got it. The command is Infinite Chains!" replied Jeff in an assuring voice, as he held his breath and quieted his mind.

"Infinite Chains!" shouted Sera.

As soon as she did, the chains of her scythes detached themselves and flew out to everyone holding aggressive intent towards her. Once the chains reached their targets, they wrapped around them and tightened up like a rope. Looking down from an aerial view, it resembled a steel spider web. Then, her weapon returned to its normal form, with all Sera's combatants stuck like bugs.

"Now you can catch my dinner for me!" Jeff chuckled as they ran away.

"Hey, Sera! Nice moves!" shouted Kai from a distance, accompanied by the rest of the team.

"Sateer could you please pick us up ten miles to the South?" asked Cullen over the communicator.

"You got it. Is everyone still alive?"

"Who do you think we are?" replied his students.

"What do we do now?" asked Kai, stressing out and pacing the room.

"We're going to find a place where no one will find us. Start over as it were," replied Cullen.

"It has to be just our crew for a while, guys," added Fang.

"Do you have a place in mind?" asked Sera.

"If I did, then it wouldn't be secret. Now, would it?" replied Cullen.

"Why not do a random warp?" asked Sateer.

"If we go too far from developed planets and our ship goes down, we'll be stuck forever!" screamed Cam.

"What choice do we have?" asked Jeff as he pressed the button to warp.

"WAH!" yelled all.

"We were going to do it anyway and you know it," said Jeff as he crawled back over to his web.

"This planet is amazing! Complete wilderness and not a human settlement in sight. I say we settle down here," clamored Cullen, while peeking out the window.

"How do you know there are no humans?" asked Fang.

"Well you see I can..." started Cullen, before he collapsed and fell to the floor completely unconscious.

"Cullen, are you okay? This same exact thing happened during our date!" announced Sateer.

"Don't worry the fatigue is due to my relic," explained Cullen, as he sat up in his bed.

"What kind of relic draws that much power?" asked Sera, who looked very curious.

"I'll tell you one day, maybe!" laughed Cullen, which angered everyone who was worried about him.

"So you're sure it's safe?" asked Fang.

"Absolutely," replied Cullen.

"Looks like we're landing," concluded Rago, as he lowered the ship.

"So, find us a nice spot to build a place, Young Hunter," ordered Cullen.

"Alright, this way," commanded Rago.

It seemed that his hunter's instincts told him to follow the river until they found a suitable place to live. He noticed from space that the planet possessed all the types of terrain found on a habitable planet. It was so amazingly untouched that he didn't want to build on it. He wanted a location that had plentiful wildlife and natural resources. Living off the land seemed like the best choice.

"I think this rainforest would be best, Cullen," announced Rago after a full month of traveling either on foot or on the ship.

"Explain please," replied Cullen.

"There's a large river that runs to a nearby ocean. We could use the trees for cover in case someone comes looking. There are plenty of animals, fruits, vegetables, and the river consists of fresh water. The only manmade structures, in my opinion, should be a spaceport and a camouflaged house big enough for all of us," lectured Rago.

"Sounds good to me," replied Cullen looking very impressed.

Chapter 7: What's the Point Again?

Their peaceful home was a little rough for the time being, but improvements could always be made. Everyone felt their creativity flowing, since their rooms had so much space. Kai had a small training circle in his room, especially since he still longed for Sera. Rago practically lived at the spaceport, so he wound up actually living there. Always the simple Hunter, he preferred to sleep in a hammock. The rest of his stuff just cluttered the corner from which his hammock hung. Cam's room didn't change very much, except for the kitchen she wanted built so she could learn how to cook for her team. Sera who loved her books begged for a physical library, but Rago wouldn't allow the slaughter of trees for the attainment of knowledge. Instead, Sateer surprised her one day with a state of the art galactic archive, which could constantly update itself with the most recent information from the Free Worlds, autonomous worlds connected by a richly large economy, network. Besides that, her taste in decorating her room stayed the same. Cullen and Sateer's room reeked of everything Sateer. Cullen did end up setting up a large shrine for his prayers in a corner of the room. Fang was content with the bowl and basket Sateer gave him long ago. He was quite the low maintenance wolf. Jeff lived out in the wilderness wherever he felt like, so he never had to go hungry. He would still check in on Sera on a daily basis, of course. Akiko and Cheri lived in their partner's room since they resembled the typical weapon that never left their partner.

"I think it's safe to say we've all just about settled in. Now, I want you all to explore the planet on foot. I want each of you to pick a place that suits your personal preferences, mark it on your map, and report back to me. Go as far as you want and take as long as you want. Oh, let's just say we'll bring the ship over and resupply you once one of you find a spot. Then, you can redeploy and repeat. Each time you need to stay together," explained Cullen.

"Questions?" asked Fang.

"Yes, what is our ultimate goal?" asked Sera.

37

"If I told you, it would spoil the adventure!" laughed Cullen along with Fang.

"Me, Cullen, and Fang will just be sprucing up the place while you're gone. Good luck kids!" finalized Sateer.

"I was still fixing up my place," pouted Cam.

"I hear you. I wish I could have put up most of my posters," replied Kai.

"You guys weren't getting bored at all?" asked Sera.

"There are always modifications to be made on the ship," replied Rago.

"I'm —" started Jeff.

"Hungry, we know!" replied all.

"No, I was going to say. I'm feeling something strange coming from that waterfall over there," said Jeff as he pointed his leg.

"I've scouted this area a million times and have never seen that waterfall," stated Rago in a confused voice.

As they walked over, they noticed that the pool of water at the bottom looked surprisingly pure. It almost sparkled with a magical sort of blessing attached. The cliff from which the water came from stood at least 30 stories tall. For some reason the surroundings made perfect sense in terms of what would co-exist with a waterfall of this magnitude. In other words, this waterfall seemed to belong here.

"Let's go for a swim!" suggested Cam.

"That's a great idea. It's so hot out today," replied Kai.

Sera already stripped down to her under garments and dove in. Everyone else followed shortly after. They all swam and played around feeling a bit like normal teenagers for a while. After they were done, they decided to set up camp for the night.

"Wow. The moon is so beautiful tonight!" noticed Cam.

"Was it that big before?" asked Kai.

"There's another one over there," Sera pointed out.

"Very astute of you. Welcome young ones to my wondrous traveling waterfall. Its waters rejuvenate the weary and heal the wounded. Enjoy the fruits of my generosity, for I will be gone in the morning. As a bonus I offer a special invitation to brave women who seek power to dwarf a raging volcano or a twisting hurricane," spoke a whimsical sounding old man's voice.

"What do you guys think?" asked Cam.

"Go for it," replied Rago with his tan skin and shaggy brown hair that went down to his ear lobes. By this time Rago stood at about 6 feet, while Kai was only 5 foot 8. However, Kai had better muscle mass than Rago who was on the skinny side.

"I'll do it," blatantly stated Sera who was swimming around with Kai at the time.

"Very well," replied the spirit.

Suddenly Sera and Kai started to feel a whirlpool underneath them, which before long engulfed the entire pool of water. They tried to swim away, but it didn't matter because a few seconds later Sera became pulled into the abyss.

"That wasn't a very polite way to invite someone into your domain wise spirit," stated Sera, as she attempted to dry herself off, except she couldn't because she was underwater. Not only that, but her form was that of a goldfish.

"Who said I was a wise spirit? You may address me as Great Demon Jiku," replied a terrifying old man with the blackest eye's Sera had ever seen.

"You may have tricked me, but all I need to do it pass your trials to be free of your realm," replied Sera in her usually calm attitude.

"You do not show your fear, but I can sense it. You may make it after all," replied Jiku.

"So how do I get out of here? You must tell me."

"Don't forget that I'm a demon."

Sera looked around at her surroundings. The visibility made it hard to see very far due to the darkness. There were strange whirlpools scattered all over the place. All sorts of fish inhabited the environment. Luckily no shortage of tall kelp existed because there were some large predators. Crocodiles and other large fish big enough to gulp her up in one bite awaited her foolish travel. She figured that she would check out one of the whirlpools to see what they were about. Once near one such whirlpool, Sera opted to spit out a piece of kelp into it to see what would happen. It floated into the whirlpool and popped out over by another.

"This is my means of getting out!" she yelled in victory before covering her mouth, so she wouldn't attract the attention of the crocodile swimming overhead.

"My my. What a tasty looking fish. What kind of fish are you anyway? You smell so delicious. Hey guys! Check out this fish over here!" hollered this smaller crocodile that awoke from her nap within the kelp.

All shapes and sizes of crocodiles swam over, while doing their equivalent of licking their lips. Sera made a break for the whirlpool and when that one didn't get her out of that horror of a situation, she went for another and so on. After ten or so tries, she hit the right one and appeared in her human form in another room. A huge crowd of people were cheering and clapping after she appeared. What kind of sick joke was this for Jiku to put her into a stadium? The crocodiles that chased her arrived as well in human form. Weapon stands lay against the walls of the circular field about the size of Sateer's ship, a large house. Sera, now in a terrible mood decided not to grab a weapon and destroy her adversaries.

One of her favorite techniques she had been developing over the years took the form of a variation of Cullen's Blur Step, Trick Step. She ran over to her first target and began attacking. She missed with one of her jump kicks and received a sword slash to her torso. At that moment she held her breath and closed her eyes imagining her next destination. When she opened her eyes, her imagination became a reality. The unsuspecting crocodile witnessed his sword slicing through a stuffed doll in a comical likeness of Sera only to feel a non-lethal explosion. The other crocodiles looked at each other and some went on to fight, while others sat on the sidelines.

Shortly after her first victory, the remaining crocodiles that were brave enough to take her on were unable to fight. Looking around the field, some were trapped in hardened foam, pinned in place by spikes that shot out of the ground, knocked out by sleeping powder, or laughing hysterically to the point of intense abdomen strain. In short, the Trick Step has a random effect every time. You never know what will happen.

"Is this all you've got?! If so, then let me out already!" shouted Sera breathing heavily from exhaustion.

"I can't believe you made it! AH! Just take the relic and get out," announced Jiku in frustration.

"You're making me go with this skinny bitch?! What are you sending me for?! Send the bear! She needs a thug!" ranted the cutest little demon wolf pup.

"Just suck it up and get out of here, Angelica. You're free now, aren't you?" replied Jiku.

"You're so cute! So, what can you do?" clamored Sera.

"You want to know what I can do. Check it," replied Angie.

"No way, twin kodachi's?!" replied Sera, as she started swinging them around.

"Cool, right? My right fang can cut though anything in the universe and the left one will send anything and anyone it touches into the storage district of the demon realm. After battle you can organize who or what you send there by talking to me. Leave the item or person in question there, delete, or kick them out back to where you first warped them," explained the beautiful little arctic wolf with a snowy white pelt.

"Are we going to get along with you being a demon wolf?" asked Sera.

"Of course. I'm a nice enough wolf, but my demonic soul will attempt to corrupt you," replied Angie casually.

"What?"

"Don't worry about it. I can sense your pure soul."

"Oh, thank goodness!" said Kai, as he rushed to Sera's side, once she and Angie emerged from the pool of water.

"Hey there. I'm Angie, nice to meet you too," said Angie feeling left out.

"Your relic is still summoned?" asked Kai.

"I'm a demon relic. I don't go away and you can't get rid of me. So get used to it!" sassed Angie.

"That explains the black eyes," added Rago relaxing by the fire.

"Oh, you're cute. Is this your man Sera?" asked Angie.

"No, he's my pilot," replied Sera.

"Just your pilot?" asked Rago.

"And my guide," added Sera.

"Harsh," stated Cam.

"Who's miss goody two shoes over here?" asked Angie.

"That's my teammate Cam," replied Sera.

"I don't think I like you!" pouted Cam.

"Demon," pointed out Angie.

"Well, we better get going. None of us have found a suitable environment," stated Rago.

"Could someone fill me in?" asked Angie.

"Why not this place?" stated Angie.

"I thought it would disappear in the morning. Also, isn't it owned by Jiku?" replied Sera.

"Not anymore. Since you cleared his trial he was kicked out of this waterfall and now it's permanently anchored to this realm. Have you notice the second moon is gone?"

"That's right. How about the changed landscape?"

"That's permanent."

"Okay then I'll just call Cullen over to pick us all up."

"So you have a relic too?" asked Cullen.

"Demon relic," added Angie.

"Of course. It's nice to meet you, Angie," said Cullen with a smile.

"Eclipse, why don't you come over?" growled Angie.

"Your nose never fails till this day, Angie," replied a deep and quiet voice, starting to take the form of a baboon.

"How did you know?" asked Cullen.

"Your soul smelled unable of being corrupted. That can only mean you have already mastered a demon relic," replied Angie.

"Close, he can't corrupt my soul anymore, but I have a long way to go before mastering his powers," said Cullen, while scratching his head in embarrassment.

"Also you lied to us. You already knew exactly where and what we were doing," accused Angie.

"How so?" replied Cullen with another smile.

"It was faint back then, but now I'm sure Eclipse was there the moment me and Sera exited the cave," said Angie.

"You're very skilled for a pup. I'm glad to have you on the team," replied Cullen.

"Garr, me too. Nice place you've got here," replied Angie, letting her guard down.

"Come on, let me show you my room!" said Sera as she beckoned Angie to follow.

Chapter 8: Do I Have a Chance?

Another quiet moment at the house made the newest resident irritated. As Angie looked around the grounds she witnessed Kai and Sera watching a documentary about seafood on her archive's impressive projection shining on her wall. She walked over to Cam's room where she and Akiko were absorbed in trying out a new recipe for tree frog leg stew. Cullen and Sateer were over at the spaceport finishing their list for the next off planet supply run. Angie didn't bother going to find Rago, since he walked out into the wilderness that morning as usual.

"Isn't there anything for us to kill?" asked Angie as she walked into Sera's room in boredom.

"Just relax a little. Aren't our lives busy as it is?" replied Kai, as he chomped on a cracker he almost choked on from laughing at how people could stomach eating caviar.

"I guess I'll just take a nap," said Angie, as she yawned and lied down next to Sera's lap.

Sera and Kai just finished a crime syndicate movie marathon, when Angie suddenly woke up and leaped off the couch in an alerted state.

"I smell a strange presence coming from the spaceport!" barked Angie, as she bolted towards the door.

"Nothing to worry about, Angie. We apprehended the stowaway," said Cullen.

"A stowaway? Come on! A stowaway requires the crew not being aware of his or her presence," replied Angie.

"Fine, I allowed her to come with us. Is that better?"

"Yeah. So what's the story?"

"This poor girl was forced into prostitution by the Knife, a powerful syndicate at the commercial planet of Serum.

"I can't believe I got away. Thanks, Cullen," said Stacey, who looked terribly hungry and weary.

"Don't mention it," replied Cullen with his ever shining smile.

"Here, let's get you to a nice hot bath," said Angie.

"Cullen, why is this little wolf talking to me?" asked Stacey, as she started following Angie anyway.

"I'll explain everything along the way," answered Angie.

Sera and Kai were still hanging out where Angie left them except Kai was snoring on a pillow, while Sera read a news segment.

"Who's that?" whispered Sera, as she saw Angie guiding Stacey down the hall towards the baths. She got up and started to follow noticing the new arrival. Stacey had worn red hair tied in a pony tail, fairly tan skin, and emerald eyes. Her figure seemed more developed then both Cam and Sera's. Sera actually felt a little jealous since she was so pretty, even in her worn state. She felt her stomach ache for some dinner, so she went over to Cam's room to see if she was cooking anything.

"Sera? Where are you? I guess she went to the bathroom or something. Ooh, I wonder if that other sitcom is on," said Kai to himself.

"Oh, who might you be? I'm Stacey. Cullen and Sateer saved me earlier today," said Stacy, as she introduced herself and walked into the room.

"Hi there I'm Kai. Want to watch a comedy?" replied Kai, trying to be nice by inviting her over.

The two of them watched until the program was over. Then, while Kai started to change the station, she decided to start something.

"Hey, Kai. Wanna have some fun?" whispered Stacey into Kai's ear.

"Huh?! Whoa! I just met you half an hour ago," replied Kai all flustered.

"Are you saying you don't like me?"

"No, it's not that. I actually have my sights on one of my friends."

"Don't you think I'm sexy?"

"Well yeah, but I like her for who she is. Understand?"

"What's going on here?" innocently asked Sera, as she walked into the room with a bowl of tree frog leg stew and some ice water.

"Kai has just rejected me," explained Stacey as she crossed her arms and frowned.

"I see," replied Sera with a stoic face.

"I was trying to explain to her that —" started Kai before he realized he was setting himself up for a love confession.

"He already likes someone," said Stacey, finishing his sentence.

"Oh? I see the problem now. Look Stacey, it seems I need to set some ground rules here," said Sera, with a smile as she walked over and grabbed Kai by the collar to kiss him.

"You two are together?" asked Stacey in bewilderment.

"We are now," replied Sera, who immediately went back to kissing her new boyfriend.

"I thought I never had a chance," said Kai, while looking up into those beautiful white vanilla eyes.

"I was always yours," replied Sera, who got up and pressed the button on her remote to close the door to her room.

The next morning, Rago was sleeping in inside the spaceport's hangar when he heard some clunking and clanging coming from inside Hope's Arrow. He woke up feeling groggy and started walking over to check out all the commotion.

"You know what time it is?" asked Rago as he yawned and rubbed his eyes.

"Its noon already, you lazy butt!" echoed Stacey from inside the ship's engine room.

"You better not be breaking anything. I worked hard on that engine," replied Rago, nearly awake.

"Well, you either made it better, which is sad. Or you completely screwed it up."

"Excuse me? Do you even know what you're doing in there?"

"I hope so. I was trained at the Imperial Academy."

"Which one?"

"The Fulmer's."

"Really. What did you do there?"

"Mechanic's Research and Development."

"What class?"

"First."

"Impressive. I was a pilot at the Venhingean Empire's academy. Second class."

"Venhingean scum. Just kidding. Did you guys hate us as much?"

"Of course. It was drilled into our skulls."

"Wanna see my ship? What am I saying? Of course you do," said Stacey, as she clicked the button on her key that she drew from her pocket.

"Oh, let me open up the hangar door real quick."

A few minutes later, a sharp looking ship resembling a grappling hook with an engine instead of a rod landing next to Hope's Arrow. The bubble cockpit sat at the front of the ship. The rest of the ship was clearly built for aerial combat.

"Never seen a Fulmer ship like this," stated Rago.

"Let's take it out. Show me what those scum taught you."

The two of them got in the tiny cockpit, which could only seat five including the pilot. Rago looked around the inside at the controls, which were surprisingly few. The only visible control was the stick used to steer the ship.

"Here put on this helmet," said Stacey as she handed him a simple and light looking helmet clearly not meant for protection.

"Welcome to the user interface for the Fulmer: Class 1 test fighter. Feel free to call me the Piercing Talon. All commands usually found on a typical ship can be accessed through your neurological functions," explained the ship's Artificial Intelligence.

"Thanks, what do I call you?" asked Rago.

"Shipia," reluctantly replied the AI.

Rago slowly looked over at Stacey knowing full well that she thought of that stupid name for the AI. He thought and commanded the engine to start and so it did.

"Great, now take me on a tour around the planet. What's this place called anyway?" asked Stacey.

"We haven't named it yet. It might already have one. Who knows," replied Rago, as he commanded the throttle to go at max speed.

"Wahoo! I know how to build them. What do you think?"

"This is great. It's so much easier to fly. I can concentrate on my steering because of this helmet."

"I was the queen back at the academy, until the syndicate scooped me up. Luckily, I managed to hide my key in a safe place. I picked it up right before Cullen rescued me."

"It does seem a bit dusty. What do you say we give it wash?"

"Sure, take us back."

The two hit it off right away, since they had so much in common. They washed and polished the Piercing Talon while talking about their days at the academy. Both completely disagreed with the philosophies being taught at the academies, but loved working with space ships.

"How old were you when you left?" asked Stacey.

"Thirteen. And I got kicked out."

"Oh that makes sense."

"What about you? Would you still be there if the syndicate didn't enslave you?"

"Probably. This ship was my life. I could keep working on it forever. They let my class have access to any resources required. Sure, I was building a war machine, but it was mine."

"I understand. Sometimes you have to deal with what you got."

Sera, Kai, and Cam walked into the hanger and immediately noticed the new ship.

"Sweet ride. Is that yours, Stacey?" asked Kai.

"Yeah, isn't he sharp?" replied Stacey with a smile.

"Yeah, it reminds me of the Assassin's fighters."

"I didn't know they had any fighters."

"They only use them for defense. In case anyone is stupid enough to invade their world, that is."

"I see. They sound old, since no one ever attacks them."

"They are. They run purely on mechanics from the old days,"
added Sera, remembering an excerpt from an old history book on
modern space craft technology of the Assassins.

"We came to tell you that breakfast is ready. Me and Akiko
made crocodile and river fruit omelets," announced Cam.

"I found it on the culinary station," added Akiko.

"Did you make my cricket cakes?" asked Jeff.

"Of course!" chirped Akiko.

Chapter 9: I'm the Strongest!

"What do you say we all fight each other tournament style?" proposed Kai.

"Why don't we all just enter in the Intergalactic Open Tournament?" replied Sera, as she walked out of her room, turning off her archive's projector.

"The prize?" asked Rago.

"A vacation to one of the resort planets. Winner's choice," replied Sera.

"I'll definitely enter then," decided Cam.

"You should all enter. Just wear some sort of costume to hide your identity," said Cullen as he puffed in out of nowhere.

"Ah!" screamed Stacey, who dropped her bag of snacks. She had never fallen victim to Cullen's sudden appearance before.

"The rest of us will cheer you three on," said Sateer as she walked over from the common room.

"The four of us," corrected Rago.

"I didn't know you could fight," stated Sera.

"That's because I'm usually in the cockpit," replied Rago.

"No weapons. Only for the Assassins of course," added Fang.

"Someone better remember to feed me from the stands. I need to be able to watch Sera's fights," pointed out Jeff.

"I'm betting on Sera," said Cheri.

"No way! Cam is going to win!" chirped Akiko.

"I don't know, Rago might surprise, you all," warned Jeff.

The stadium that held the tournament didn't exist on a planet, but on a huge spaceship near the Free World's economic center, the world of Centyen. The ship had the utmost amount of security, made obvious by the blockade circling it. All sorts of ships arrived at the hanger bay. This event was one of the most broadcasted events in the universe. Even the two empires were allowed to enter for the big occasion. Some fighters proudly represented their home and nation, while others kept their anonymity, for various reasons. The anonymous contestants were largely accepted and left alone, even if they won. For this reason, it was perfectly okay to allow the kids to compete in Cullen's mind. Plus these were the best in the universe. The kids registered their names and were assigned numbers. After the brackets were all set up, they went to their respective waiting rooms.

"Would our first two fighters enter the stadium!?" requested the announcer.

"Do it, kid!" hollered Cullen, while the others added their own cheers into the mix.

Kai readied himself and got into his fighting stance. He bowed to his opponent who gave him a traditional Free World's salute.

"Begin!" cried the announcer as the crowd went wild.

Kai's opponent decided to play it cautious and wait for his younger adversary to initiate the battle. Taking the hint, Kai rushed in with a flurry of test kicks in order to see his man's skill level. All of them were blocked or dodged, which gave Kai the impression that he had a good fight on his hands.

"For the Free Legion!" shouted Kai's opponent.

"We honor you, General Danton!" replied a large section of the crowd.

Danton seemed to be a respected person among his people, but because of his position Kai forgot about holding back. This time Danton charged with the presence of a raging bull. The ground seemed to quake under his feet. He threw a mighty haymaker in an attempt to end things right then and there, but Kai grabbed it and threw him. Sadly his throw barely got the job done and Danton was largely unfazed, especially with his enormous muscle mass. Too bad Kai couldn't cut through him with Cheri. He tried to weaken him with some quick jabs to the ribcage and kidneys, but all was for naught. Danton finally grabbed the boy by the neck and tossed him ten feet across the ring. Sitting on the edge of the circular ring, Kai knew the only path to victory was to knock him out of the ring. Kai feigned being hurt by writhing in pain. Danton smirked and triumphantly raised his arms into the air.

"Finish him our, great general!" chanted his men.

Danton nodded to the crowd and slowly walked over to Kai who lay in wait. Once Danton drew close enough, Kai kicked him in the gut, sprung up, and push kicked him out of the ring. The crowd grew furious after the tricky maneuver he pulled off. Danton got up off the floor and jumped back onto the ring with a seriously intimidating display on his face.

"Calm down, everyone. This boy didn't break any rules. I should be the one being booed at. I was the one who underestimated my enemy. I hope all my soldiers learn from this," lectured Danton, honoring his defeat.

The mood turned joyous as the crowd responded to Danton's admitting of defeat and Kai walked back into the waiting room thankful for not being stoned to death.

A few hours later, after the tournament went through the other fights, it was finally time for Sera's first match.

"Moving on to our next match! Will the competitors please enter the field?! We have a member of the Assassins and an anonymous fighter! Begin!" rallied the announcer.

Sera in her usual aggression rushed her opponent hastily. This Assassin had no problem with using his techniques in this fight, which was legal as long as no lethal weapons were used. Once Sera saw that he summoned his axe in a blunt state, she requested the use of the weapon's rack. Grabbing a kodachi from the weapon stand was new for her, but she wanted to practice because of Angie. This man in his thirties had seen his days out in the field and it was evident in his axe wielding. Sera nearly received a heavy swing after getting too close. She ducked and sliced at his foot only to see him jump up into a front flip. While spinning in the air in order to add momentum to his downward swing, the crowd rose to their feet in anticipation. Sera rolled right under him before the bearded axe struck the ground. Taking advantage of his brief vulnerability, she attempted to hold her blade at his throat to force a submission. This turned out to be foolish since he grabbed her wrist and tossed her across the arena. He decided to disappear and give chase. Sera wasn't about to lose for not using her own powers, so she figured disappearing as well wouldn't raise too many suspicions. It takes years of experience for two Assassins to fight each other, while invisible. The fighter who had the best ability to mask their own presence, while on the prowl, would come out on top. Luckily Sera's master had this down to a science. The trick, at least in Cullen's opinion, was misdirection. Use any means necessary to disturb the environment in order to either fool your opponent or give away their position. Sera stirred up some dust and darted off as fast as she could. Then she made some noises here and there. At the same time, she kept her ears and eyes open for anything out of place. Then, she heard it, but unfortunately she was just too lacking in experience.

"It seems I've caught you, little Assassin," laughed the man, as he lightly squeezed her neck.

"You're good. What gave me away?" replied Sera.

"That pattern of attack could have only come from Master Flint, but his student is older than you. I know you're Cullen's student. I also know that the council has been looking for him and his team for some time now. I don't know why, nor do I care what you're doing here, but it was a bad idea. I won't say anything, but don't take off that costume no matter what," said the Assassin before slamming her onto the wooden floor of the ring.

Sera nodded in appreciation after slowly getting back onto her feet. The man threw his axe at her, which caught her off guard. Then, she saw his weapon transform back into its animal form, a wild boar. It started to charge and so did its partner. This style was rarely seen, but in a competition without casualties, it made sense. Sera decided to focus on the man instead of the beast for the time being. She decided to trip him up by throwing her weapon too, but she accidentally threw it out of the ring. The audience laughed and Sera turned red, but then Angie jumped up onto the ring.

"Don't worry, I'm her weapon!" stated Angie.

"Why were you on the rack!?" asked the Assassin.

"We thought those were the rules," replied Angie, hoping he'd buy it. He didn't.

"Alright," replied the Assassin with a sigh.

"Sera you get the boar, I'll take this guy," ordered Angie.

Sera didn't want to get yelled at by Angie in front of the entire universe, so she listened. Angie growled at the big guy, bearing her fangs. She went and used them to chew on his leg, while Sera grabbed the boar by his tusks. She threatened to rip one off, but the boar begged her not to.

"We'll switch our weapons back and finish this fight normally. Agreed?" proposed Sera.

"Fine," replied the Assassin.

Sera felt that it was obvious that she was an Assassin for a while now, so she wasn't going to hold back. She gave Angie the signal for the left Fang. The Assassin sensed that she had activated something, so he too used his relic, God of the Air's Messenger. A gust of wind surrounded his axe, making it look awfully intimidating. Sera timidly walked over toward the man who pointed his axe at her. A second later a small tornado shot out at her. She managed to dodge it, but she would have been knocked out of the ring. Sera couldn't think of a way to get close, but then she had it. She rushed in straight ahead without the least bit of hesitation. Once the next gust came at her she cut it with her the Left Fang, which made it warp. The Assassin knew he was in trouble at once.

"I admit defeat!" announced the Assassin.

"The Assassin has given up. The winner of this match is the anonymous fighter!" said the announcer as the crowd went crazy at the recent turn of events.

"We did it!" cheered Sera.

"Damn right!" added Angie.

After a few matches, it was Cam's turn to fight in the Quarterfinals. At this time she had already defeated a few competitors. She felt confident enough to keep winning.

"Would our next two fighters please enter the ring?" shouted the announcer.

Cam walked up to the ring and to her surprise, so did Rago.

"Don't worry, I'll go easy on you," stated Cam in a friendly demeanor.

"Thanks, but you haven't seen me fight," replied Rago.

"Begin!" shouted the announcer.

Cam encouraged Rago to try his luck with a hand gesture. Taking the invitation, Rago jumped up and disappeared. Cam couldn't believe her eyes as she looked around at her surroundings for Rago. Then, a thunderous kick came down towards Cam's head. His heel would have demolished her skull, if she hadn't sensed it in time. A shockwave of electrical energy pulsated from the point of impact. Cam got caught by it and became stunned temporarily. Rago took advantage of her temporary vulnerability and continued his onslaught by jumping again. The next time he reappeared, he elbowed Cam in her gut. The force of the impact overwhelmed her and she lost consciousness.

"Cam, are you okay? Wake up! I didn't think I could hurt you like that," said Rago filled with concern.

"It's okay. I couldn't prepare myself since I was still stunned. Where did you learn that? You didn't use it in your previous matches."

"It's a long story. Maybe I'll tell you once I win!"

"Oh brother. I can't believe you kept something like that to yourself all this time!"

As the tournament winded down to the last three fights, with the last being the final bout. First up were Rago and Kai. Kai had seen what Rago had done to Cam, who should have won in every way due to her training. He wanted to avenge her and prove that Assassin training stood second to none.

"Begin!" shouted the announcer.

Rago could see the ferocity in Kai's eyes, so as soon as the match began he immediately jumped into the air. Once Kai saw this, he threw one of his wind potions onto the ground to create a temporary gust of wind around him to repel Rago's incoming attacks. When Rago reappeared, he received a powerful pushback from the wind. After Kai had seen Rago hit the ground, he let his opponent get up to give him a chance to see his next plan of attack. Rago bumped his fists together and summoned electricity which surrounded his body like a suit of armor. Kai knew this had to be some sort of equalizer, so they could fight fifty-fifty until his potion wore off in about two minutes. Rago went in and started trying to knock Kai from the spot where the wind was aiding him. The two of them traded blows and tried to break each other's stances down and find a weakness. Kai managed to stand his ground for the remaining duration of his potion, but Rago still had enough energy to keep up his armor. Kai knew that if he received a hit, he would either be destroyed on the spot or paralyzed for a while. Either way, he needed to keep his distance. Kai didn't know this, but Rago was running low on energy. Despite this fact Rago wanted to try to end it because sooner or later Kai may pull out his Katana. Kai had a lot of fine qualities, but in terms of speed he couldn't dream of matching Sera or Cullen. Lucky for him, it was impossible for Rago to disappear and wear his electric armor simultaneously. Kai could have used his shield, but he didn't think this situation called for something that would drain his energy so much. After a short while, Rago knew his plan could not produce a victory for him. Instead he called for the weapon's rack. In his mind, he had worse skill with weapons, but maybe he could find a weakness.

"You sure you want to do this?" asked Kai with a cocky smile.

"Shut up."

Kai drew his sword and started with a flurry to test out Rago's skills with his tomahawk and knife. A tomahawk wasn't the best defense for a katana, so Rago was forced to do a great deal of dodging and countering. Kai really started to wear down Rago, who was starting to lose confidence in his abilities.

"I think it's time I finish this before I embarrass you too much," announced Kai, as he sheathed his sword and got into a draw stance.

Rago's eyes widened because he knew this was Kai's specialty. Thinking quickly, he figured that he had just enough energy to pull off something desperate. Kai stared his prey down when he tossed up his tomahawk high up into the air. This distraction naturally caused Kai to look up. While Kai started to look back down, Rago threw his knife at Kai. Now Kai started to draw his sword in order to deflect it, but it was interrupted by Rago's unrelenting kick to the back. Kai who had been distracted twice went flying, while Rago caught his knife followed by the plummeting tomahawk.

The crowd must have cheered louder than it ever had in more than a century. The climactic ending to the semi-final bout proved to be one for the record books. Sera had gone on to win her Semifinal match. Both Rago and Sera received a day to rest up before the Final.

"It seems you barely made it past Kai," stated Sera, as Rago left the stadium.

"How do you know? Your match was at the same time," replied Rago who stopped to sit down next to her.

"I saw the recording and studied your moves," replied Sera, holding up a tablet.

"Trying to get an edge on me?"

"You know me," replied Sera with a smirk.

"Kick his ass for me, sweetie," added Kai, as he was being taken to the medic in a stretcher.

"I will and don't call me that. Think of something else!"

"Sorry," replied Kai. He asked one of the nurses for a pen and piece of paper.

"For what, dear?" replied the nurse.

"For exactly that. I wonder if she would like dear."

"Oh no, that's more for married couples."

"Hmm, good point."

"THINK ABOUT IT LATER!" hollered Sera from down the hall.

Everyone was relaxing back on the ship the day before the Final. Cam and Kai were still recovering from their injuries, which were nothing to worry about. Even though Rago didn't pull any punches.

"It looks like you can expect a full recovery in about a week. Remember not to strain yourself," explained Sera, while looking at Kai's medical reports. Kai was lying on her lap, watching his favorite show. "I don't understand your fascination with this program," stated Sera, while she pet his head.

"I just love sitcoms," simply stated Kai. He got up to stretch and get a drink from Sera's fridge. "Want something?"

"Water please."

"Cullen has an announcement, you two" said Fang through the door.

Everyone gathered in the common area to hear the announcement. "I did some looking around during the tournament and the last few fights caught the eye of the Assassins. It doesn't look like they know it's us, but they are definitely watching closely," explained Cullen, as looks were exchanged around the room. Some were full of worry and others with confusion. "My advice is to not worry about it. If any complications arise, I'll take care of it."

"Aren't you taking this too lightly? What if something happens to us for showing powers that are obviously Assassin taught?" asked Cam.

"Just don't worry about it. I have a plan. Just go all out and have fun," replied Cullen with a smile.

The crowd was as invigorated as ever for the Final to start. Sera spent the previous night putting together her strategy. She made sure to go to bed early so that she could fight in top form. Rago on the other hand did not make many preparations. He felt confident in his abilities that he had yet to unveil. Everyone took their seats except for Cullen, who was impersonating a beverage vendor in order to keep a roaming view on any possible Assassin movements.

"Today, the moment we have all been waiting for is upon us! The Final! Today's match is between two anonymous fighters. One with an electrifying personality and the other with a cool yet aggressive ferocity. Now without further delay, let the match begin!" said the announcer, as the crowd's excitement grew in anticipation.

Both fighters took their stances and stared each other down. Sera wanted to wait for him to make the first move so that she could lay a trap, but he was no fool. "I need to do something to draw him in," she thought. "What are you waiting for, an invitation?" she goaded Rago.

"Do you really think I'm that stupid? Fine I'll attack first." He ran up and prepared to punch Sera, who smiled.

She waited for the impact so that she could Trick Step to set a trap, praying for a good one. His punch was just about to reach her when he suddenly pulled it back and activated his Static Field. Then, he simply flicked her forehead and she was still there without an explosion or anything.

"What did you do? I couldn't teleport," asked Sera in frustration.

"My Static Field keeps you in this realm, the Visible Realm. Your Stealth abilities temporarily put you into the Shadow Realm.

Since I can't go into the Shadow Realm, I'm at a disadvantage, unless I use this," replied Rago.

"So I can't go invisible either."

"Exactly."

"It can't last forever."

"True, but this fight will be over soon enough."

"Angie, Warping Kodachi."

"It's about time," replied Angie feeling anxious.

Sera went forward and sent a flurry of kicks and punches at Rago who successfully fended them off. She never tried to slice at him with the Warping Kodachi. He jumped up and tried to teleport to catch her off guard, but he had to be careful not to accidentally get sent into another dimension.

"I need to finish this soon. I'm running out of energy. If she gains her Stealth back I'm done for," thought Rago.

He jumped back and concentrated his energy into his right leg, which began to glow with radiant golden energy. Sera saw this and knew she needed to think of some sort of countermeasure. Rago jumped and disappeared, and then all of a sudden the whole audience heard, "Thunderclap Kick!" shortly followed by a huge boom that echoed for miles. A huge crater appeared at Sera's location. Once the dust settled, there wasn't a trace of her left.

"Infinite Chains!" shouted Sera from the other side of the arena. Rago suddenly became entangled like a helpless little fly.

"This is impossible! Everything in that crater should've taken damage. Where did you go?" shouted Rago as he foamed at the mouth.

"To another dimension. You see I didn't have much time, so I stabbed myself with Angie, who safely placed me into another dimension. From there she brought me back away from the crater. I can use Infinite Chains as long as Jeff remains within earshot," explained Sera. All the while, Angie stood next to her nodding condescendingly.

"That's right little boy. You thought you could defeat a demon and her subordinate," bragged Angie.

"Oh shut up, mutt," replied Rago.

"I'll ignore that for now."

"One, two, three," counted the ref, who really didn't need to finish.

"Our winner is the female anonymous fighter!" shouted the announcer.

On the winner's podium Sera was awarded her vacation to a premium resort planet. She bowed in appreciation and decided to give a little thank you speech. "I appreciate the prize, but I would like to let you all know that the best part of this entire event was to bring joy and excitement to your lives. It was an honor to be here. I could actually use some cash instead of a vacation, so I'm willing to sell my vacation to the highest bidder. My user name is The Champ on Centyen's intergalactic bidding service. Oh, and I still can't believe I won!" spoke Sera. The crowd ate up her speech and some started to go on the bidding service right away on their devices.

"You did it, sugar!" said Kai as he went to give her a warm embrace.

"Thanks, just don't call me that."

"Sorry to break up the love, but we need to get out of here. Before that, does anyone want a cold drink?" added Cullen, while acting like his usual lighthearted self. He was disguised as a drink vendor.

"I have the ship ready for takeoff," added Sateer.

"So what's the rush?" asked Jeff. "I'm still hungry," he complained as he rubbed his belly with all eight legs.

"Don't worry about it. Cam and I bought you some flies at the kiosk.

"The chocolate covered ones?"

"Of course!" said Cam with a smile.

"One of the Assassins disguised as a reporter wants to interview Sera," explained Cullen.

"How did you find that out?" asked Cheri from Kai's neck.

"I wish I had time to explain."

Everyone arrived in front of the ship where Stacey was waiting with a relieved look on her face.

"We have a problem guys. I picked up an Assassin fighter hiding in stealth on my scanner," warned Stacey.

"It has to be her ship," guessed Cullen. He started to pace pensively.

"Do you think she's on it?" asked Stacey.

"You think she has a pilot?"

"If so, then they might be ordered to give chase for so long before coming back to pick up the undercover Assassin."

"Where are you going with this?"

"I can disable the ship while you guys take off. I have enough fuel for one warp. I'll see you guys at home.

"Okay. Be careful."

"I'm coming with you," insisted Rago.

"Be glad to have you," replied Stacey with a wink.

Chapter 10: Narrow Escape

Sateer went full throttle, blasting out of the spaceport at
breakneck speeds. The authorities didn't care to chase them. They
were still watching the highlights of the Final of the tournament.

"Captain Denise the target has passed right by me,
permission to engage," radioed in the ship's pilot. She was two years
Cullen's senior and a brilliant tracker.
"Are you sure it's them?"
"Yes, Tim confirmed it was her who entered the ship."
"Did he place a tracker on the ship?"
"Unfortunately not. Their leader seemed to be on to us."
"Please pursue them. Either disable their ship or place a
tracker on them before they warp."
"You got it. Ben out," ended the pilot, as he started after the
Hope's Arrow.
The Hope's Arrow kept its course heading for nothing in
particular.
"Do you have your suit on nice and snug?" asked Stacey. She
helped Rago with his spacesuit, making sure that his helmet wouldn't
come off or anything.
"I think I'm ready to go. This is insane, but it'll definitely
catch them off guard.
"One, two, GO, GO, GO!" ordered Fang, as he pressed the
button to jettison them out of the ship's airlock.
The two of them shot out into the cold of outer space at an
incredible rate. At that moment Stacey activated the key for the
Piercing Talon to pick them up.
"What? Captain, two people were shot out and have entered a
fighter. Ah! On top of that the cruiser has just warped. Please
advise," radioed Ben, as the Talon commenced engaging his ship.
"Capture that fighter!"
"You got it. Over and out," ended Ben.
Stacey started to shoot at the other ship's wings or engines,
being as careful as possible not to pierce the cockpit. A couple well

placed shots was all she needed. Rago already knew that she was a skilled engineer, but her flying was almost as good as his. Unfortunately, Rago was not familiar with the controls of her ship. In this situation, she was their best shot. The Assassin pilot knew all sorts of maneuvers that she had never seen before. She had her hands full with this one. The dogfight went on in favor of the Assassin for the next few minutes. The Talon took a few hits to the body, but nothing serious.

"Something's not right. He clearly outclasses us. Why hasn't he disabled us?" wondered Rago. He ran a diagnostic on the ship. The amount of shots that landed on the ship should have done more damage. "I say we get out of here. Lead him somewhere and try to lose him."

"Fair enough. Here, you take over the controls for a while," replied Stacey. She got up and pulled out her tablet to run a more advanced scan on the ship. "Shit he stuck us with a Remote EMP!"

"That can't be good," replied Rago. The ship started to shake and then something blew, along with all of their electronics. "I must have set it off." He was humiliated by his poor piloting.

"It's not your fault. He wanted to trick us into running. That smart son of a bitch!" yelled Stacey.

A loud thumping sound hit the hull and they started to move. A towing line attached to a magnetic end now pulled the helpless ship along.

"Hasn't it been a while? They should be back by now," said Sateer in a worried voice.

"You're right it looks like their tracker has been removed. We have to assume the worst," replied Cullen.

"But we can't go back with our ship. They know what it looks like now."

"That's okay all we have to do is rent one."

Stacey awoke after a rush of ice cold water soaked her body. After looking around she could not see Rago. She assumed he was in another room.

"I'd like you to fill me in about you and your friends. Why go through the trouble of breaking the Assassin's rules? They're there for a reason," asked Captain Denise. She walked up to her and looked into her eyes. She could tell that a great loyalty had been instilled into Stacey. This interrogation would not go smoothly.

"Can I have something to eat please? I might be more inclined to talk," replied Stacey. She knew it might be a stretch, but feeling out her adversary was her main goal.

"I don't see why not. Is a sandwich alright?"

"Yeah that would be great!"

"Captain we have a ship requesting contact," notified the pilot of the cruiser.

"Patch them through," replied Captain Denise.

Cullen came up on the screen without his mask. Denise's eyes widened upon seeing his face.

"Looking good there, Nice," said Cullen with a chuckle. Her fair face with short black hair turned red as if she would catch fire. "Don't look like that, Nice, it doesn't suit you. Don't let this job get to you."

"Are you telling me that you're the leader of these rogue Assassins?" replied Nice in disbelief. She didn't know what to do. "You were like a little brother to me. How could you do this?"

"Look, can I come on board so we can talk this out in private?"

"Fine, go ahead and dock."

"You think I'm stupid enough to join you? I have a career. My team relies on me. I have more people under my command than you, therefore I have more to lose," ranted Nice.

"Out of anyone I know back home, I trust you the most. Haven't you ever felt like being an Assassin does no good for the universe?" rebutted Cullen.

"He has a point, Nice," added Lucy, her snow owl weapon who takes the form of a sniper rifle.

"As lovely as ever, Lucy," said Cullen.

"Thank you my dear. What about your nightmares?" replied Lucy, as she turned to Nice.

"Fine, let me sleep on it. But in the meantime, stay docked to my ship, you can have your people back, and we'll discuss this in the morning." concluded Nice.

"Sounds good, goodnight," said Cullen, as he went to release Rago and Stacey.

"Before we get things started, I'd like you to meet my team. Just the Assassins for now. The rest of the Intel personnel will come later. Come on out guys," stated Nice.

Three eighteen year old Assassins appeared from stealth. This did not surprise Cullen and the gang especially since they were spies.

"I'm Tuco, our stealth and medical expert."

"Hey! Rina, I'm the enforcer. Nice to meet you."

"Eric, I arrest suspects with various traps."

Everyone got to know each other better, while Cullen and Nice discussed the situation. The spread at the table had everything you could want. Nice's cruiser was bigger than Sateer's since it had to accommodate her full staff. "I haven't eaten this well in a while," said Cam, as she hastily ate some pancakes drenched in syrup.

"I guess fugitives don't have the luxury of normal food," added Eric.

"Are you trying to start something?" started Kai, as he abruptly stood up.

"All of you are about to be arrested soon anyway," replied Eric, getting up himself.

"Now now, I think they support a noble cause. Please enjoy your breakfast guys," interjected Rina.

"Fine, but I'm not gonna pretend like I support all this craziness," said Eric, after sitting back down.

"So why go through all this trouble? Do you not believe in the teachings you grew up with?" asked Tuco.

"Once your leader is on board, I'm sure you'll understand," replied Sera plainly. She patted Kai on the back in order to cool him down.

"We help people instead of killing them. What's not to like?" added Cam.

The room stayed extremely tense for the rest of breakfast. It was tough for Cullen's team to describe their motivations to these people who never second guessed their upbringing before. There were a few attempts to break the tension, but Kai and Eric were still about to brawl.

"You will have my full cooperation and all of my resources will be at your disposal. However I want all of the decisions to go through me. By this, I mean I want an important position on your team. I want to have the peace of mind that my services are being used for good," stated Nice, in a very diplomatic manner.

"Awesome! Trust me, you will not be disappointed by your decision. What are you going to do about quitting?" replied Cullen, who lit up with enthusiasm followed by worry.

"I'll just disappear. It's fine. The Assassins are more worried about tracking you guys down."

"Let's go tell the others."

The cafeteria was in tatters when Cullen and Nice returned. Kai and Eric were engaged in unarmed combat. They were both bloodied up from the fight. It seemed like a sanctioned match at this point, though certainly not at first. The two read the situation and decided to watch.

"Not bad for some sixteen year old," admitted Eric, while wiping the blood from his mouth with his sleeve.

"Thanks you really know your stuff. I thought you would be someone who hides behind his traps," replied Kai.

The two continued by exchanging blows. Kai tried to throw him, but he blocked it and kicked the side of his rib cage. This did some damage, leaving him reeling. Eric took advantage by going for the knockout punch, but Kai just smiled and threw him into some chairs.

"Ring out! The winner is Kai!" announced Rina, as she motioned for Tuco to check if Eric was alright.

"I can't believe he won. Eric has excellent hand to hand combat skills," stated Nice in awe.

"Guess I'm just the better teacher," bragged Cullen, while putting his arm around her.

"I should kick your ass like back in the day," replied Nice, as she grabbed and twisted his arm.

"You can try. Ah, ouch!" replied Cullen, who had his arm twisted even more.

Chapter 11: Expansion

Cullen and Nice's ships landed at his base's small spaceport. Luckily, there was just enough room to accommodate both ships. However, there weren't enough rooms for everyone. This made Nice happy because it meant that she could be creative in building for her team and herself. She decided to simply build near Cullen, only a few miles down the river in case she wanted to expand her facilities. She didn't want to impose, so she decided to use her own funds for the construction. She got her men working on the project and they were happy to. Reason being she was a great leader.

Her men were not recruited in a typical way. She went out of her way and personally interviewed each candidate. They were not necessarily the best at their craft, but she looked for potential and character. They were grateful for the fact that she went through the trouble of giving them a chance when others wouldn't.

"Cullen, I don't think we can help people enough with this small a fighting force. We might get snuffed out one day," stated Cam.

"That's a good point, but we definitely can't have an army," replied Cullen.

"How about a specialized fighting force that can strike at critical points?" suggested Fang who came back inside from a run.

"Is it safe to recruit new people? Some of our newbie's might turn us in." added Akiko.

"Good point!" replied Cam.

"Thanks! I try," said Akiko as she landed on her shoulder.

"We'll kill the ones who betray us," said Kai from around the corner. He walked over and started clashing his fists together.

"No killing, Kai. You know that. I'm not budging on this," replied Cullen, looking agitated.

"Isn't our cause worth a few lives?"

"We're trying to save people. We can't do that as Assassins."

"Then what are we?' asked Kai raising his voice.

"I don't know, but we're not killers."

"Then why did we kill back on Formota?"

"That was the last time!"

"Remember that when our backs are against the wall again!" cried Kai in frustration. "Look at what we have here. It's so great. I don't want to think about how things would be if I lost one of our own because of your stupid rule! I need to get some air, excuse me," ended Kai, as he hurried out into the rainforest.

Kai had been walking into the rainforest for a while. He lost track of time as his emotions overwhelmed his state of mind. Cullen's cause meant everything to him. Kai felt that his teacher did not take his council seriously enough. Sometimes the evil needed to be rooted out. He had tasted blood many times and he had killed both good and evil people. It felt good knowing a drug lord or human trafficker met their end. He couldn't understand why Cullen didn't understand this.

"You're right, boy," growled a dark voice inside Kai's mind.

"Who are you?" replied Kai not in fear, but on guard.

Suddenly a giant brown bear appeared before him in spirit form. He seemed to be kind and wise, if a bear's expression can show such things. Kai felt comfortable as he walked over and sat down.

"I'm a spirit of this forest. Not the guardian. Just an old bear. Ha-ha!" said the bear in an introduction.

"I'm Kai, nice to meet you. So why are you talking to me?"

"Humans are more interesting. I used to be the weapon of an Assassin. About 500 years ago now. My partner was lucky enough to die of old age. So did I. I'm Grizz by the way."

"Wow I didn't know this could happen. So what should I do?"

"Don't get me wrong, your teacher has a point. For what you're trying to accomplish, killing should be avoided. The only thing is Assassins are ruthless. I'll say no more. I can't just tell you. Come with me. I want to show you something." He motioned for Kai to follow him.

The two of them went deeper into the rainforest than Kai has ever gone before. Then, they passed through something. It turned out to be an illusion type barrier leading to a grave.

"Who's this?" asked Kai. He walked over to the headstone and examined the name. It read, "Here lies beloved Assassin and partner of Grizz, Tolas."

"That is your ancestor," said Grizz with a warm smile.

"What did you just say?" asked Kai, grabbing the bear's arm.

"He was a good man. Tried to do what you're doing now. Until... Gosh it's a tough story tell," started Grizz who scratched his head. "The man trusted too much like your teacher. Let me show you." As he finished, the two were taken into the past where an older Assassin stood with his student.

A secluded room on an unknown planet only contained the noises of a stove heating a pot of tea. A young woman about the age of 20 looked down with remorse.

"Why would you tell me this? You know where my loyalties lie, where yours should too. I don't know what to say. Give me a reason why I shouldn't turn you in," said June in much distress.

"I expect nothing from you, but your honest opinion. By now you know me well enough to trust me as much as I trust you. I have a good feeling that you will do the right thing," replied Tolas.

"I need time to think about this," said June before leaving the room.

"Tolas, I'd like you to come with me. There's something I want to show you," said June with a tear in hear eye.

"So you're turning me in. It looks like I didn't teach you to think for yourself," replied Tolas, as he walked toward the door.

"You're being cruel, Tolas," added an Assassin officer.

"I guess you can't destroy evil with a gentle hand," declared Tolas.

The old man of 70 summoned his hand axe for the last time. The officer was startled to see such swiftness, but he never forgot who he was dealing with. Tolas sunk his axe into the officer's spine before long, but soon after June knocked him out while sobbing.

"He spent the rest of his days rotting away in a jail cell with a broken heart. He really believed in June whom he trained since she was only thirteen. She was top of her class, a shining star among her fellow Assassins. Maybe that's why she couldn't betray them," explained Grizz.

"I can't believe it. How come I've never heard about this?" asked Kai, as he wiped the tears from his face.

"It was never recorded in the history books and understandably so."

"I think I get why you said that I was correct."

"What did you learn?"

"That I need to be the one to protect my friends, but I need to go along with my teacher for now."

"Good job. Tolas would be proud," said Grizz, who patted Kai on the back. "Listen, since you are my partner's progeny, you can talk to me anytime you'd like. Meditate when you have some alone time and I may even be able to channel some power to you from Tolas," explained Grizz.

"What exactly are you talking about here?"

"Just wait until the next time we make contact. I'll return you to where we first met," finished Grizz.

Kai started to head back to the base. Along the way he thought hard about the lesson Grizz tried to teach him. How could anyone fathom being betrayed by your most trusted friend? At the same time June clearly showed remorse. Who was right? Conversely, was anyone right? All of these issues swam around inside his mind. His ultimate conclusion told him that everything comes down to fate. He would do what he felt was best and live with the results.

The base looked a lot more like a developing city. A speed rail connected Nice's buildings and Cullen's. People and supplies could now be moved at great ease. Nice also had her own space port. It definitely made for a momentous first. Nice had her three students, two ace pilots out of the Assassin's exclusive flight school, five Intel officers from a non-Assassin company, and two engineers. All made Cullen's cause that much stronger.

Chapter 12: Back to Formotia

Nice and Cullen were sharing a breakfast conversation, when Fang and Rago walked into the room.

"We think that we should sneak on down to Formota and see how they're doing," stated Fang.

Rago walked over and sat down next to Cullen.

"I'm worried about my dad. It's been eating away at me for a while now," added Rago. He looked at both of the former Assassins for some sympathy.

"I don't see why not. What do you think?" asked Cullen, who got up to put away his dishes.

"I think it's a great idea. I'll send someone down there first to make contact to let your dad know we're coming. I can tell you this. They've had their hands full trying to keep the Venhinge Empire from taking over again," explained Nice.

"Thank you so much, the both of you. Please let me know when you get word," finished Rago as he left.

"I'll go with your men to make sure things go smoothly," added Fang, who started towards the door.

"Hold on. Sit, stay!" said Cullen only half jesting.

"You know I hate that," replied Fang, who knew Cullen wasn't happy.

"Do you not trust Nice yet? You've known her as long as I have. Lucy as well," said Cullen. He felt like kicking Fang.

"You're too trusting Cullen," said Fang.

"What now? You too? Trust me I know Nice would never betray me."

"I hope you're right, for all our sakes," said Fang who shook his head and sighed.

The cruiser arrived above Formota, it looked different than before. The biggest difference being the lack of Venhingean ships patrolling the area every once in a while. The smaller shuttle ejected and landed on Rago's old home of Ixue. Security guards escorted two intelligence officers and Fang to see Tergen.

"Ah Fang, it's good to see you. Where is Cullen?" asked Tergen, who was happy to see Fang.

"That's strange. You've never seen his face. Also, you know him as Night," replied Fang. He immediately sat down and waited for what he knew would come.

"That's a good boy," said Eric. He opened up his pack to pull out a sleep inducing collar. Fang calmly sat there as the traitor's student confirmed his hunch.

"Cheri, I need to find out if Nice is really on our side," said Kai. He got up to summon Fuu.

"I think you're wrong, but I like how you stand on your own two feet now," said Cheri, as she slithered up and around his neck.

"You called? Don't you want Rai?" asked Fuu after yawning.

"I didn't get a chance to really meet you. Can you help me with something today?" requested Kai.

"Sure, I suppose. Let's see. You want me to see if Denise has good intentions. Let's go then," said Fuu. She started out towards speed rail to visit Nice.

"Wait, how did you know that?" asked Cheri.

"Part of the overall power of influence requires one to be able to enter another's mind. Luckily you chose the only one of my siblings who can do that," explained Fuu. "Looks like we're here," said Fuu, before transforming into a simple white ear ring on Kai's right lobe.

"What do I do?" asked Kai, as he approached Nice and waved.

"Just chat with her for five minutes and by then I'll have scanned her mind," explained Fuu into his ear.

"Good evening, Kai, what can I do for you?" greeted Nice, with a tablet in her hand. She had been reviewing the plans for new computers to be used by the Intel unit.

"I just wanted to spend some time with my teacher's so called 'Big Sis'," explained Kai, while trying not to sound so nervous.

"Fair enough. Do you happen to know anything about computers? I want to get something fast, but I also don't want to burn through my budget. Would you care to take a look?" implored Nice.

"I know enough. Hmm... These ones are a bit expensive due to the brand name. I would go with these. Here," said Kai, returning the tablet to Nice.

"The Z010? Never heard of that model," stated Nice, while looking skeptical.

"Oh that's got to be my favorite line of computers, Captain," said an Intel officer, who just happened to pass by.

"Really? Well that's good enough for me. Thanks kid," said Nice, as she messed up Kai's hair.

"You're very welcome," replied Kai, who was actually starting to like her.

"OK, I'm done. She checks out. There's nothing in that noggin' telling me that she's a traitor," reported Fuu. After hearing this, Kai parted ways with Nice and walked towards the speed rail.

"Thanks. Hmm... That still doesn't change my uneasiness," replied Kai. He rested his chin on his hand and thought about what was missing.

"I'm tired. I need to go take a nap. Until next time," said Fuu who disappeared.

Kai made it to the speed rail. He had to wait fifteen minutes until the cargo was unloaded. He was just about to sit down on the bench, when Lucy flew over to him.

"There's trouble Kai. The Intel team along with Fang hasn't reported back. We also can't find Eric anywhere. Come quick, dear," announced Lucy the snow owl.

"You were a liar from the beginning. I can't believe I trusted you," said Kai, seething with anger.

"I'm sorry. I don't know what you're talking about. Is there something wrong?" asked Nice in confusion.

Kai simply summoned his katana showing his readiness to attack. Nice immediately rose to the occasion. Her cover had been blown. She didn't know how it turned out this way, but now this young man who rushed towards him meant business.

He opened with his favored draw stance, which grew since his first training session with his teacher. She was nearly caught off guard. The room left little room for dodging. Her sniper rifle could not help her in this situation. She went for the door, which Kai wouldn't make easy. A poisonous cloud of smoke filled the air. He only inhaled a small portion of it, making him a little dizzy. That turned out to be just enough for her to make it out of the room. Upon recovering he quickly gave chase.

Fang awoke in a cage looking not very surprised at all. He had lost all hope of escaping anytime soon, when a large thump alerted him. Upon surveying the area, he noticed someone force the door open. After seeing the guard plop down onto the floor, a familiar face stepped over him. It was none other than Sera.

"Come on, we need to get you out of here."

"How did you find me?"

"I hid in the ship. Did you really think I trusted Eric?" replied Sera, after picking the lock on the cage door.

"Look out!"

Sera rolled out of the way of whatever she had just been warned about. It turned out to be a knife thrown by none other than Eric, only this time he was accompanied by Rina. Sera looked at Fang who knew exactly what to do.

"All's Eye!" shouted both Sera and Fang. At that moment their left eyes turned black with a star in the middle that shone bright like a sun.

Eric and Rina looked a little fazed before deciding to attack. Fang moved in to attack Rina, who would make things more difficult in the long run. Sera covered him by blocking the handful of throwing knives flying at Fang. Rina raised her brass knuckles and threw an explosive punch at her attacker. He just barely managed to dodge it, however the next one connected.

It was not a complete loss because Sera managed to scratch her with a numbing poison. Rina angrily looked at Eric, but he shook his head in a way saying he tried his best.

Needless to say, the enemy wasn't in good shape at this point. Unfortunately, a certain someone came out of stealth.

"Sorry I'm late, it looks like the rest of the Assassins are on their way. It won't be long now," said Tuco, who just kicked Sera hard in the back.

"That's why we tagged along as well" added Rago who practically announced his own arrival like a prize fighter. A big flash filled the room as one of Cam's grenades blinded everyone except her allies.

"How is this possible? When did you call for reinforcements?" asked Eric in seething anger, while still trying to regain his sight. Once he did, it became evident that every one of his enemies had the same golden left eye. All's Eye allowed everyone on Cullen's team to share sight and mind while active. It only takes one member's activation to do the same for everyone else. That is how Fang and Sera fought so effectively as a team.

"Where do you think you're going!" yelled Kai, who sent a small tornado towards Nice with a swing from his sword.

"You think you have me?"

Her sniper rifle finally flew down and transformed to aid her. Kai just realized that going outside into the forest may not have been the best idea. She ran over into some of the trees and out of sight. He needed to think of something and quick. Meanwhile, he dodged the sniper shots the best he could even though a couple connected.

Reaching into his pockets for something useful led him to a crazy idea. Why not dump all of his elemental potions onto Cheri. It wouldn't last very long, but it might just be enough to make a difference. Two fires, one lightning, three waters, and one wind, all assimilated over Cheri's blade. She cried out in agony.

"It burns! What did you do to me!" yelled Cheri. Suddenly she felt something sooth her pain. All of the elements absorbed into her snake skin and turned into a bright multicolored aura.

Kai recognized the surge in power giving him a signal to swing his blade. All the energy exploded out towards Nice's general direction razing the entire section of the forest. It wasn't only fire, but the other elements as well. It was as if every natural extreme caused by weather struck all at once. The earth stood a compete wasteland.

The nothingness started to settle in and Kai felt Cheri fading. She transformed back into a snake. "I need to rest. It seems I shed my skin after that last attack."

"No problem, I'll think of something."

Nice shot another bullet, which pierced his leg this time. His knee wouldn't be doing him any good for the rest of the fight. He summoned Shelly to help him.

"Good choice, at least for now," commented Shelly, who just materialized.

Kai closed his eyes and tried to listen for the slightest hint at her location. He heard the trigger pull. He could not tell where the shot originated, so he jumped up and spun in the air in a way that provided the most coverage. Thankfully the bullet hit his turtle shell shield, causing Nice to feel a painful bite. Soon after, Nice fell from the tree, hitting branches the entire way down. She broke her arm. By the time she got up, Kai had managed to make it over to her location.

"Ok, I give up. I surrender."

"You're not getting away with that one. I won't let you get a chance to escape," he said, as he raised his combat knife high. With a swift stab, the Captain who caused so much grief for him and his comrades lay dead. With a sigh of relief, Kai took a rest underneath a tree providing ample shade.

"Do you see anything on your scanner?" asked Cullen, while peering over Stacey's flight controls.

"Not yet, but if what Tuco said is true, we need to keep our eyes peeled," replied Stacey.

"Something has arrived on the edge of the scanner's map," reported Shipia.

"Here we go. I'll take you up to the flagship."

"Thanks, Stacey. I want you to stay inside the cockpit. We might want to leave in a hurry. Scratch that, we will definitely be —" explained Cullen, expecting the worst case scenario.

"Don't worry, I got it covered, Boss." Stacey confidently reassured Cullen with a thumbs up.

A tone indicating a request for contact between ships alerted Stacey to patch them through.

"Hello this is General Mutia. I'd like to speak to whoever is in charge of this vessel."

"Speaking sir," replied Cullen, trying to sound official as well.

"We received a call to capture this vessel and detain its personnel for the murder of several Assassins on the planet Formotia."

"That would be us."

"I understand that there are more of you currently engaging more Assassins on the planet's surface as we speak."

"That would be correct sir."

"Would you care to cooperate or do we need to prepare for an open conflict."

"Let's meet face to face."

"Please dock when ready. See you shortly." The session ended and Cullen nodded at Stacey to begin docking.

Once on the ship, Cullen actually noticed a lot of familiar faces. Some of his old classmates were scattered here and there. He wore his mask to try to keep his identity a secret, but the crew called out to him. The words that erupted along the way included traitor, idiot, fool, and dead man. Basically, everyone knew that it was Cullen behind the mask.

"So here we are. I never expected you to become a full blown —"

"Traitor? Yeah I know," said Cullen, who finished General Mutia's sentence.

"Do you know what happens to traitors?"

"Their locked away for life."

"Exactly. Except for one thing. You also cease to exist."

"Come again?"

"You're erased from history. Upon death, anyone who ever knew you simply... won't."

"I'm happy to tell you that will never happen. You know why? Because I'll die before you capture me."

The General got up and summoned his bastard sword. The man stood only two inches taller than Cullen, but his physique suggested he could wave that large sword like a wand. "I think you underestimate your former brethren."

Still sitting in his chair, Cullen took his music player from his pocket, which really enraged the General. The first swing broke Cullen's chair and echoed through the air creating a sonic boom.

This being precisely the reason for Cullen putting in his ear buds. The attacks were meant to deafen unsuspecting attackers. After hand springing himself back onto his feet, Cullen opted to select a good fighting playlist. The General couldn't take it anymore, but as he would soon find out, he had a better chance with his opponent still picking his music. Getting into his rhythm allowed Cullen to regulate his heart rate and concentrate better on the fight.

An elbow coming in at mach speed struck the General on the side of his neck. After managing to shrug it off, he swung his sword again. This time Cullen just barely dodged the sword swing, which prevented him from being unscathed. The boom churned the insides of his opponent's stomach and made his ears ring despite the ear buds. Cullen spat out some blood onto the floor and coughed. Feeling nauseated, it became difficult for him to see straight. He pulled out a small vial from his pocket and drank. It contained a concoction he called Dragon's Venom. It harshly burned his insides, but after vomiting he felt refreshed. It served as a temporary cure for the fight to come.

At this point, not having a weapon proved too much of a handicap. His only other option would be to activate his relic. He kneeled down on one knee for a second to request aid from Eclipse.

Inside his mind, he called out, "Is there any kind of combat support you can give me?"

"Seal me within a part of your body and I'll see what I can do. Choose carefully because that part will become my new home."

"Fine. Let's see. Take my left arm." Cullen decided hastily.

He felt an immense presence envelop his arm. Then it turned black with a silver lining. It didn't really look like it consisted of flesh, but developed scales which formed a vambrace. The next strike delivered by the General's bastard sword literally blew up in his face. The vambrace absorbed the attack and reciprocated it with a push, which sent the general flying into the wall. The energy of the push matched what it received.

"I like this! What else can it do?"

"Try absorbing a few attacks and releasing energy as you punch," replied Eclipse, from within his new home.

Cullen waited for the General to recover before testing out his new toy. The once life threatening battle just turned into an experiment. After blocking an entire onslaught of attacks and almost getting taken out, he decided to try it out. He tried to focus the energy he stored up into his knuckles. The pain from holding onto it started to take its toll.

"Keep it up. If you let go of it, you'll be the one to take the damage."

He tried to activate stealth, but it wouldn't work. Neither did his Blur Step. It looked like there were drawbacks to the technique. Running as fast and he could and drawing ever closer to his enemy made his hand hurt even worse. The General wasn't about to go down easy. He readied himself for a huge homerun swing. Without having the time to dodge the incoming blade, he decided to punch it instead. The resulted blast shattered the blade into shrapnel all the way down to the hilt. The pieces tore through its former partner who met his unfortunate end. Cullen fell to his knees in horror. He didn't know he would unleash that kind of power. With a crushed soul and a possessed arm, he wondered if it was all worth it.

"How should we proceed?" asked Sera. She stared down the enemy back on Formota. The short break wasn't going to last much longer.

"One second," replied Cullen from the enemy flagship. He got onto the microphone and addressed the crew of all ships under the command of the now deceased General. "Attention all Assassins, this is Cullen. I'm sure you know by me contacting you, your leader has been defeated. I give you only one chance to either join me or die. Once I leave on my ship, I will start the self destruct sequence on all ships who have not complied. All who send me their ship's identification codes will be spared. You know the rules of engagement and my requests are in compliance with said rules. That will be all."

Cullen put down the microphone and began his way back to the Piercing Talon. Most of the Assassins along his way saluted him in recognition. He didn't see any more disgruntled Assassins and that gave him some peace of their mind. One quality of the average Assassin was their respect for power. To them they did not see a traitorous coward, but a fearless warrior. He shone with an unbreakable will which pulled them in with gravitational force. Few could deny that to defeat a seasoned veteran such as General Mutia was no small feat. All but a few of the smaller ships chose death over joining Cullen.

"Your teacher's dead. You might as well give up as well," said Cam to Eric and his team.

"What? Who killed her!" replied Eric in a horrific rage.

"Kai," replied Rago in all seriousness.

"You'll pay for this!"

"Don't choose death. You've lost," replied Cam trying to quell his fury.

"Let's get out of here," added Tuco as he placed him and his team mates under his stealth.

"Well that takes care of that. Let's return to the ship. Something happened to Kai. Can anyone else pick him up on All's Eye? I don't see him anymore," said Rago with concern.

"He's not coming through on my end either," replied Sera.

"Well let's get going!" added Cam hastily.

Upon opening his eyes, Kai coughed up some blood onto the snow covered earth. His body felt so cold that it could shatter like a sheet of ice at any second. After regaining more consciousness, he noticed that he was being carried. He couldn't free himself, although he tried.

"Hey! Let go of me! Where am I?"

"You're on Sultura. Now go back to sleep," replied his mysterious captor.

Chapter 13: The Aftermath

Cullen landed back on the base where he met with the rest of his team, except for Kai. No one knew where he went to. He ordered all of the ships who joined him to restock and refuel until further notice. He wasn't sure if it would be a good idea to allow them to land at their base quite yet. He would deal with them later. Right now, the top priority was finding Kai. He told Cam and Rago to go with Stacey in her ship to look for any clues through rumors around at some popular refueling stations with heavy traffic. He, Sera, and Sateer would do the same on Hope's Arrow.

"Do you guys have everything you need?" asked Stacey. "It's going to be a while. I don't think we'll be able to find him today."

"I'm ready to go when you are," replied Rago. He sat down after putting his things in the storage compartment.

"I just need to grab a few more schematics and parts from my room. We don't know what we might run into out there," said Cam apologetically. She ran back to her room as quickly as she could. A few minutes later they had made the warp for the Kitous Fueling Station.

The station which floated out in the middle of space near one of the Free Worlds supplied a lot more than just fuel. Weary travelers could get a well cooked meal, have a drink at a bar, and do some quick shopping for the essentials or the occasional black market goods. The criminal underworld thrived in refueling stations such as these. Information brokers and bounty hunters provided their services for surprisingly fair prices. The prior was what interested Stacey.

"I need to pick up some spare parts, you guys go see what you can find," said Stacey, once the ship was safely docked.

"Ok I'll hit some of the bars and see what's up," replied Rago, who looked at Cam. "What about you?"

"I think I'll try the security offices and wanted person's terminal." Cam looked at a map of the area.

"Sounds good. Let's just meet here at 6 pm," added Stacey.

"Careful guys!" yelled Akiko who flew into Cam's hood.

"Where do you think we should look first?" asked Sateer. Her ship sat out in space just outside the atmosphere of their base's planet.

"Hmm... maybe over at this checkpoint. Plenty of traffic passes by here, especially since it lies between the Venhingean Empire and Free Worlds territories," replied Cullen. He looked at a map on his tablet.

"What about the nearest refueling station besides the one Stacey's ship went to?" added Sera.

"Good point —" started Cullen until the console rang. Sateer answered the call.

"Sir, you have a call from Master Dacard," said one of his new recruits.

"Ah! I mean, yes put him through," answered Cullen. He cleared his throat and started to sweat.

"Cullen, this is Dacard. How goes it?"

"How goes it? Aren't I a fugitive?"

"About that. The council and I have decided to cut you a deal. We will allow you sovereignty as long as you promise me a few things."

"I'm all ears sir."

"We want you to make sure whatever you do from now on doesn't take anymore action than what the Assassins do currently. I mean you can go on your little crusade as long as you don't destroy the universe."

"Why allow this?"

"We all know you and what you're capable of. We trust you won't turn into a tyrant and slaughter millions of people with the training we gave you. Also you followed the rules of engagement and fairly conscripted some Assassins. If we can agree to this, then the Assassins won't be at war with themselves."

"I understand sir. Can someone still hire you guys to kill me?"

"Of course, but don't take it personally."

"Let me consult my advisors for a second," said Cullen, as he turned and looked at Sera and Sateer for their opinion. They both looked at each other and nodded as if they didn't expect any kind of deal like this in the first place, so why not?

"You've got yourself an agreement sir. So where do I sign?"

"I'll send you the link. I'll just need your digital signature."

"Ok. Oh there it is. Did you get it?"

"One second. Yes. Well, that'll do it. Until next time."

"I hope not, sir. Goodbye," ended Cullen. He ended the call and sighed in relief.

"I would be skeptical of what you just agreed to," noted Sera. She rested her chin on her palm and thought about what happened. "I think you we should watch out for spies within and outside our ranks."

"She's right. I don't think you should let your conscripts on our base," added Fang after he turned back into a wolf.

"I can place some trip wires around our base in case someone is already snooping around. For a price," said Jeff.

"How does a bag of dark chocolate crickets sound," replied Fang with a grin.

"You know me all too well. I actually placed them a long time ago."

"And?"

"What's his name, the stealth kid from Nice's team snooped around? I don't know what he found, but I didn't think anything of it at the time. Sorry, guys."

"It's alright. At least we know you can tell who touches your webs."

"I'll set course for the checkpoint," said Sateer. The ship came to life and warped. Shortly after a smaller ship turned off its camouflage and landed on the planet surface.

"You alright, sonny boy?" asked an elderly woman, with smoke coming from her mouth.

"Oh I'm feeling better now. Thanks Grandma Yalo," replied Kai. He stretched and slowly got up from his sleeping bag. Cheri decided to sleep in and coil up in the sleeping bag. She wasn't fond of the cold weather.

"Good, now help your brother catch some fish for lunch."

"What about breakfast?"

"You slept through breakfast."

"You're strict you old bag!"

"Shut up and get out of the hut! Ha-ha!" she replied, with a cough after smoking from her long wooden pipe.

Outside of the hut, the snow seemed to melt a little bit from that morning leaving it less icy, but crunchy. The conditions were fair for ice fishing, although a long drill was still required to open up a hole.

"What are we catching today?"

"Whatever bites," replied his captor, his older brother, Kain.

Immediately outside of the village stood a huge lake. To the untrained eye, it wasn't a lake at all. The surrounding area had nothing but flatlands until the horizon where mountains started to form. The valley looked like the best choice for a village. The two arrived at the usual fishing spot.

"Drill here?"

"Sure, why not?" replied Kain. He didn't really seem too enthusiastic that morning.

"What's wrong?"

"I wish I had your life."

"No you don't."

"What makes you say that?"

"It's a curse."

"I have powers too. Everyone at this village does, but if we're caught using them, then we're done for."

"I know, but the Assassin's life is full of heartaches and danger. It's so peaceful here."

"You mean boring."

"Why don't you come with me?"

"No, I couldn't."

"Why not?"

"I have to teach the children."

"Oh, right."

"Explain to me why you need to waste your time with that again?"

"We're unique. Our family is the only one with one-hundred percent Assassin's blood."

"How come I'm the only one who received official training?"
"You're not the only one."
"Wait there's more? Where?"
"They're dead. Only a few are allowed every few decades."
"Oh! I got a bite! What do I do?"
"Reel it in stupid!"
Kai yanked on the pole so hard that it snapped. He pulled out a worthless pole without a string and showed it to Kain.
"I hate it here so much. Let's go back."
"But Grandma is going to give us an earful!"
"I'm not the one who broke our only string."

"What? No fish? I'm starving!" whined Kelly.
"Sorry little cousin. Blame it on Kai," replied Kain.
"Stupid, Kai! Can't you fish?"
"Apparently not."
"Kain, Kai, Get in here!" shouted Grandma Yalo from just outside her hut.
The two boys, one sixteen and the other eighteen entered the hut and sat down near the fire. Their grandma coughed and looked at both of them carefully. She seemed worried, but then she reassured herself of her decision.
"Kai, I want you to take your brother with you."
"What? I thought you need him to stay here?" replied Kai. He received an elbow to the arm for that comment.
"He needs to get out. Look at him! He's wasting his life away on this shit planet."
"Thanks Grandma —" started Kain.
"I wasn't talking to you! Wait your turn. As I was saying, I can train up another teacher myself. Cousin Urgo just needs a few more years. I can get your uncle to help me until then."
"Are you sure? Because..." started Kai.
"Thanks Grandma! He's going to help me pack right now!" interrupted Kain. He grabbed Kai by the arm and dragged him out of the hut.

"Hey baby, want to dock on my —" started the information security officer, before getting knocked off his chair by a flustered Cam. Her communicator rang and she picked it up.

"Hello?"

"Cam! Thank goodness. Why doesn't anyone pick up? This is Kai."

"I can't believe it! Are you alright? Where are you? What happened?"

"Relax, I'm fine. I was just visiting some long lost family. I'll explain later. I just wanted to tell you that I'm heading home. I'll see you soon."

"Well, I'm just glad you're safe. I'll tell the others. Ok bye." Cam activated All's Eye and let everyone know the good news. They all decided to regroup at home. She couldn't believe how Kai just rescued himself in a way, but she didn't care how at the moment.

Sera rushed over and gave Kai a kiss before everyone else greeted him as well. He filled them in on what had happened to him. They had trouble comprehending it all. Cullen above all was curious about his family. It sounded like Kain was the official teacher for his village, meaning he had to be the most powerful.

"Kain, can we spar?" asked Cullen, sounding a little too eager.

"I don't see why not. You're curious to see what a true Assassin fights like. Am I right?"

"A true Assassin?" asked Sera with a raised eyebrow.

"You'll see what I mean."

Fang led the two of them to the training arena, a typical ring with plenty of room. "Whoever gets knocked out or forced from the ring loses. Use whatever force necessary. Begin!"

"Mind if I have the first move?" asked Cullen in all confidence.

"Go ahead."

Cullen summoned Fang to his hand and went into stealth. His opponent closed his eyes and sat in a praying mantis position. A few seconds later, his eyes opened and he blocked Cullen's attempted slash to his jugular. Cullen was thrown across the ring. He would have gone out if he didn't flip and gracefully land on his feet. Feeling a bit surprised he decided to lay off the stealth.

This time Kain went into stealth. Cullen looked around with his yellow eyes and enhanced nose, but nothing could be sensed. He received a push kick followed by a hammer fist once he hit the mat. Gasping for air, which could not be caught, he was left vulnerable to the next attack. Kain exited stealth with his hand wrapped around Cullen's throat. As he picked him up, he saw his opponent dig in deep for the strength to resist and fight back. Cullen broke Kain's grasp on him and jumped back to recover for a while. The moment was short lived for Kain now summoned his weapon, gauntlets. Cullen's eyes widened as Kain rushed him with enhanced speed. A kicking back flip sent his attacker's fist upward. Instead of being thrown off guard, Kain spun with it and recovered.

By then, Cullen's blade was at his throat from behind. Kain smiled before blowing smoke out of his mouth. It entered Cullen's lungs and burned his eyes. He started to cough and grew nauseated. Fang reassured him and told him to use his senses. Kain caught Cullen with a devastation right cross. After staggering, Cullen shrugged it off and pumped himself up. He could barely feel the presence of his attacker, but the rest was being masked by Kain's stealth skills.

He decided to give himself a boost with a potion cloud. This concoction boosted both his and Kain's senses. Since his were the only ones that were impaired, it made his opponent's too strong. Kain's hearing made his head feel like it was going to explode. Also everything looked too bright. On a side note, he could smell everything, both good and bad. Now, Cullen had a chance to counter attack. Still without his vision, he used his Blur Step to dash all around Kain. All the movement and illusion made him feel dizzy, so much so that he fell to the ground. From there his relieved opponent kicked him outside of the ring like a ball.

"Wow what a great fight!" applauded Sera. She was very impressed how Kain nearly defeated her teacher.

"I really want to see Cullen lose one day. Ha-ha," added Cam, who giggled with joy.

"Close one. You'll get him next time, Kain," said Rago, clapping with approval.

"You guys are on another level!" said Stacey.

"I need a doctor. I still can't see," stated Cullen, who lay on the mat.

"Me too," added Kain.

"Some brother you have," stated Cheri, who slithered down from Kai's sweater towards Sera.

"Someone just stepped on one of my trip wires," announced Jeff. "Also where are my crickets, Fang?"

"Where did it come from?" asked Cullen.

"Let's see. I think I could tell if I had some food in my belly."

"Here's your precious cricket!" yelled Fang, as he dropped it next to Jeff.

"It came from your room." said Jeff. His mouth was stuffed with the dark chocolate covered cricket.

"But we're not two minutes away from my room!" A large boom was heard as a ship took off in the distance. "Stacey!"

"I'm on it!" she replied. She ran as fast as she could, so she could jump onto her ship already on its way. Cam, being the closest to her, hopped on after her.

"Can you catch it?" asked Cam, as she buckled in.

"Hopefully. It looks like we have a 'Class A' chaser ship."

"Kill the after burners."

"I'm trying to line up a shot before it warps." She put on Shipia to help her with the targeting.

"I suggest you fire," suggested Shippie, short for Shipia.

"Who asked you!? Fire!" yelled Stacey who was trying to concentrate. The concentrated turret shot clipped the wing and sent it into a spin.

"Nice shot!" noted Cam, who patted her on the back.

"Thanks. Now let's see what we've caught."

Cullen sat across from the mysterious visitor in one of their guest rooms. They didn't have an interrogation room yet. The person was covered in medium armor and looked like a seasoned smuggler of some sort. His helmet had a Free Legion insignia on it.

"So what is an ex Free Legionnaire doing way out here?"

"The Free Legion wanted me to check you guys out."

"I don't buy that for one second."

"It was a bounty of sorts."

"Try again."
"Fine. I'm a private eye."
"That's more like it."
"So can I go now?"
"Not quite. I don't want anyone knowing where my base is."
"How about you cut a deal and I go away?"
"Ok. How about I hire you as a mercenary?"
"Why would you do that? You hardly know me?"
"I know that you were a Free Legionnaire and they are the finest trained volunteer army in the universe."
"You know your stuff. I'll give you that."
"I'm going to put you on probation for a while to make sure you don't try anything funny."
"You're the boss, boss."
"What about you're pay?"
"You seem like a reasonable guy. It looks like you have a sweet little set up here. There's got to be money somewhere around here to pay me with."
"Thanks for the confidence. Let's go introduce you to the gang."

The new member of Team Cullen was named Lenny or Len. Although he joined in an unorthodox manner, if there was one, he seemed to get along with everyone. He decided to walk around a bit and try to get to know everyone and make himself useful. His first stop was Sera's room. He knocked on the door.
"Oh hey, Len. Can I help you?"
"I was actually wondering if you needed any help."
"Well Kai and I were just trying to check the news on Formota. Last time we were there, it looked like Rago's dad was paid off in order to trap us."
"From what I've heard, Formota does have their independence, but they are drowning in debt. They lack monetary support."
"Of course! Thanks, Len."
"Sure, is there anything else?"
"I think you've done plenty so far. I owe you one."

"Ok see you later then." He left and decided to check on Sateer next.

"Nice ship you got there," said Len. He caught Sateer tweaking some small things around the hull of Hope's Arrow.

"Really? How can you tell?"

"The outside has a shitty paint job, but you can tell from the engine's exterior that everything's in top shape on the inside."

"Good eye! Cullen couldn't see as much when he first saw it."

"Have you seen my ship?"

"The chaser? Not yet."

"Well, let me give you a tour!" he beckoned her to follow him to the spaceport. "So how long have you been with Cullen?" They left Section 1 and passed by Section 2, which held the Piercing Talon.

"Let's see. A little over three years now."

"Wow, you know that's a long time if you think about it."

"Yeah I guess so. I never really thought about it. We've been so busy."

"I understand. Well, here we are." The ship stood the same size as the Piercing Talon. You could tell the ship was built for speed. Instead of the standard two engines, it sported four turbo v-shaped engines. The v-shape split the engines, making it less crude and more efficient. It also allowed for tighter turns.

"Hmm. Not a typical Free Legion ship."

"It's my racer. I call her the Sprinter."

"Name makes sense."

"Yeah. Had to name it something. Want to see the inside?"

"Sure."

They had to climb a ladder to get into the cockpit. It seemed pretty inconvenient, but it was a racer. The controls were extremely crude. Not as much electronic assists, meaning it took a delicate touch and someone who knows the ins and outs.

"The seats are comfy!"

"Yeah, I spend a lot of time in here and it's too small for sleeping quarters."

"So you prefer to really feel how your ship handles during flight."

"What told you that?"

"Your controls are completely old school."

"Yeah, well that's how I was taught."

"Were you any good?"

"Look up the name X-42."

"Don't need to. You were the top racer for five years in a row before you quit."

"Are you a fan?"

"No. It's just that racers have the best ship parts. It's a good way to gauge which parts you want to buy."

"If you're interested in parts, I know a guy who owes me a favor."

"I could kiss you if I wasn't with anyone!"

"Don't mention it! Ha-ha."

"It's dinner time guys! Cam and I made soup in a bread bowl!" chirped Akiko who flew in wearing a little chef's hat.

"See you there. We'd better get going," said Sateer.

"Alright," replied Len. He noticed his stomach growl.

"Man I'm starved! I'm so glad it's not fish!" said Kain.

"Oh that's right you used to live in a frozen wasteland," replied Cheri.

"Don't remind me."

"We have an area just like that on this planet. You could feel right at home."

"Give him a break, Cheri," said Cam. "So how's the food everyone?"

"Not bad. Where did you learn to cook?" asked Len.

"Oh I just picked it up over time."

"*We* picked it up over time!" added Akiko, wanting credit for the cooking.

"Of course. Sorry." replied Cam.

"So what are we going to do about money, Cullen? We need to keep up this whole operation. All those Assassins need to get paid don't they?" asked Sera.

"I really have no idea this time. The overhead is just too huge." Cullen scratched his head.

"Why don't I smuggle some goods?" replied Sateer.

"That's a great idea, but is that going to cut it?"

"It depends on what you're smuggling," added Len.

"This sounds illegal," replied Sateer with suspicion.

"We are talking about smuggling here aren't we?"

"Yeah, but I smuggle food and medicine. What do you propose?"

"Alcohol, certain drugs, and people."

"I don't think so. Do you know how many bounties we'll have on our heads in a matter of days?"

"Ok how about just alcohol and people?"

"What kind of people? Convicts?"

"Refugees and otherwise displaced innocents."

"Are you really a private eye? You sound like a pretty well rounded guy. What's your deal?"

"I'm a pirate! Ok?!"

"Cullen! You hired this scum!?"

"I have his file right here." Cullen slid his tablet over to Sateer who combed through it.

"Wanted for dozens of counts of piracy in all known sections of the universe. Well, he certainly has a full resume."

"Are you telling me you already knew who I was?" asked Len.

"You're famous. A lot of my friends tried to kill you and failed." Cullen shrugged his shoulders in a matter of fact way.

"Hmm. I don't understand you, but I'm starting to like you! Ha-ha!"

"Lead us to our buried treasure then Len. I'm putting you in charge."

"Alright, here's where we need to start." He explained that he needed to retrofit Sateer's ship to make it accommodate docking the other ships during travel. They were going to get the parts from his buddy and Stacey would work with Sateer and Kain on the ship. Rago and Kai were going to help him pick up the parts on Saratous, a Free World. Cullen, Sera, and Cam were going to secure the goods and people to be smuggled.

"Do you want me to fly?" asked Sera sitting in the back seat of the Piercing Talon next to Cam.

"I can fly, just not very well," replied a frustrated Cullen.

"Just put me on auto-pilot," added Shippie.

"How do I do that?"

"Say 'auto-pilot engage'."

"Auto-pilot engage."

"Where do you wish to go?"

"Helom."

"Warping in five seconds."

The planet Helm stood on the edge of the Free Worlds. It was close to the border leading to the Fulmer Empire. The terrain was very tropical. Island chains scattered the world. A large platform famous for its shopping and trading was Cullen's destination. The Talon made its descent and landed at the spaceport.

"I'll go retrieve the list of people to smuggle. While I do that, you guys sign for the goods," ordered Cullen.

"Got it!" replied Cam.

"I think it's over this way," said Sera.

The two girls headed down the street, passing by some shops. Some seemed very intriguing, but they were pressed for time. It was crowded that day and hot as well. They were dressed too warmly for the temperature. Everyone else wore shorts or sun dresses.

"I need to grab some water, do you want some?" asked Sera pointing to the vending machine.

"Yes please."

After taking a sip of water they continued on and made it to their contact. The man handed Cam a tablet asking for a signature. It checked out and the two started to head back to where they landed. They got there and didn't see Cullen, so they decided to go check on him. When they arrived they saw him looking at the list of people to be smuggled. He was having a heated conversation with the contact.

"I'm sorry, but I have no control over who signs up. I need to go now, if you don't mind," explained the contact apologetically.

"Fine, go ahead. Oh hey guys, how'd it go?"

"No problems. Are you alright?" replied Sera.

"Yeah, you seemed mad," added Cam.

"I'm not. It's just there are so many people on the list here. They all seem to be from war zones. We're going to have our hands full. We can't possibly take them all on one trip."

"Why don't we use one of the Assassin's ships?" replied Cam.

"Of course! But won't that make it look like the Assassins are helping out?"

"We can repaint the ships we conscripted."

"Great idea Cam! You're on fire today!"

"Thanks!"

"We should make our own flag. What do you think Sera?" asked Cullen.

"Let Cam come up with the ideas," replied Sera.

With his pride injured, Cullen slowly walked back to the ship. The two girls giggled and followed.

"How are you guys doing back there?" asked Len.

"Your seats are so comfy!" replied Kai.

"It's like being hugged by your pillow," added Rago. He barely had the ability to keep his eyes open.

"Yeah, I was telling Sateer how I spend a lot of time in my ship, so I want it to be comfy."

"Smart man," replied Kai. "Forget about Rago, he's sleeping now."

"That's fine. We need to pass a few more check points."

"Why so many?"

"That's how they keep the Free Worlds safe. The more checkpoints, the less direct landings on planets after warping."

"Hmm. I get it now. I think I never noticed because Assassins don't really get that many Free Worlds contracts."

"That's because there isn't as much conflict. It's usually the two Empires putting out hits on each other."

A few hours later, they made it to Saratous. It was a very mountainous planet. Each season attracted visitors interested in action sports. Hiking and climbing especially. There weren't many big cities because of the mountains. Mostly small villages made up the landscape. Len's friend lived in one of the bigger villages called Treego.

"Wake up Rago. We're here," whispered Kai in Rago's ear.

"Hmm? Oh ok." He got up slowly and found it hard to get up from the comfy seat.

"Her house is just over this way. Just be careful not to stare too much. She's sensitive," explained Len.

"What's that supposed to mean?" asked Kai.

"Just trust me." They followed Len passed a couple of houses. He rang her doorbell.

"One second! Get off the couch, Kid, we have guests! Oh well if it isn't my deadbeat husband. Come on in."

"Why did you ring the doorbell?" asked Kai. He took his shoes off and entered.

"She changed the locks. Plus I'm a deadbeat. I haven't been home in what, five years?"

"Sounds about right. But more like five months. Maybe you just missed me that much!"

"Rago why are you so quiet?" asked Kai. He saw Rago staring at Pricilla without blinking.

"Hey! Quit staring at me pervert!" she threw a spatula at the boy right in the face.

"Sorry. I don't know what came over me," replied Rago.

"It's alright. I used to be a model. I guess I still got it!"

"Damn right baby!" said Len before giving his wife a big smooch. "By the way, I need some parts."

"Sure, just fill out an order form and I'll get it right out to you."

"You're the best!" Len handed the order form to Rago to fill out.

"Yeah, but that's not why you married me."

"Baby, the kids!"

"Oh, they know what I mean."

The two whistled and looked around the house as if they had no idea.

"These are some great parts! What do you think Sateer?" asked Stacey.

"I agree. We can do whatever we want with these!" Sateer felt so much excitement welling up inside. She wanted to start right away. "Kain, why don't you install this part for me?"

"Where do I put it? And what exactly is this?"

"You don't know what a battery is?"

"My ship is just a basic model with no customizations."

"Ok well, just assist us the best you can."

"I don't get why I'm here in the first place. Wouldn't Cam have been more useful in this situation?"

"Good point. You can hang out until she returns if you want."

"Fine. If you don't want me."

"Thanks. Oh and please close the door on your way out."

Feeling unwanted, Kain decided to go take a walk in the rainforest. He really enjoyed the scenery the planet had to offer. There was less wildlife that tried to kill you. After going a little further into the rainforest, he heard a commotion coming from a waterfall. A raccoon was growling at a skunk for some reason. Evidently the two were fighting over a scrap of food, something from the garbage. The skunk sprayed the feisty raccoon in the face. With a burning face and a lost lunch the raccoon looked rather defeated. Kain felt bad for the poor little guy, so he threw him a snack he had in his pocket. He got bored and returned to the base. As he drew closer he saw the Talon and the Sprinter land.

"Hey Cam, I was wondering if you'd like to help out Sateer and Stacey instead of me?"

"Sounds good. I have some homemade equipment they might like!" She raced off to her room to grab said inventions.

"Oh hey, little guy! Did you follow me home? Come on in!" He motioned for the raccoon to follow him inside. Once inside his room he set down a blanket and pillow. A few minutes later he came back with a food bowl and water. The raccoon seemed to have already made himself at home on his bed. "It looks like you're going to be trouble. Ha-ha. Come on out and say hi Lucy." A white cat came out from his pocket.

"He says thanks for letting him stay here. Sorry he can't talk yet," explained Lucy.

"You'll help me teach him won't you?" asked Kain.

"Of course! What did you see in him anyway?"
"I don't know, but I was right about you. Right?"
"I suppose."
"What's his name?"
"Kyle."
"You can call this your home, Kyle."
"He's taking a nap now."
"Alright, let's go check on the others."

"Yeah, I need you to lend me a large transport ship. Great thanks. Don't worry I'll give it back to you in one piece. Yes, I won't paint it anything too weird," said Cullen to one of his Assassins, before hanging up the communicator. "Man these guys are too attached to their ships!"

"They get reprimanded for losing or damaging them, so it makes sense," replied Sera who took a bite of her steak.

"It sounds like everything is in place then?" asked Len.

"Yeah we should be ready in two days." replied Cullen.

"Hold on there! We're not done with the ship yet!" said Stacey.

"I have a couple more gadgets in production!" added Cam.

"Aren't you always building something?" asked Kai.

"Don't hamper her creativity," whispered Sera.

"Is one more week a reasonable time frame for you guys?" suggested Fang. He ripped a big piece off his wild turkey leg.

"I think a couple of us should get over there early and scope out the place. Make sure we don't have any unwanted visitors," suggested Angie.

"That's not a bad idea. Let's go with her Kai," added Cheri.

"Ok. Anyone else want to join us?" Kai looked around the room.

"Oh, me! I want to go!" volunteered Kain.

"Kyle wanted to go too," said Lucy. She almost choked on her piece of fish.

"Fine, but I'm in charge! You got that!?" barked Angie.

Kai finished packing up all of his gear on the Sprinter. Angie was anxious to get going, so they were taking off early in the morning. Kain, almost as eager as Angie, looked up the planet they were going to drop off the refugees. Sutok had a reputation for being one of the nicest Free Worlds. It had a very supportive government. Medicine, work, and education were easily attainable. The climate was also very habitable and could easily support a large population. That much couldn't be said for other planets. All in all, it was a wonderful place to live. The only problem was the strict immigration laws, the screening process to be exact.

"What are you wearing?" asked Angie.

"This is typical for citizens of Sutok," replied Kain.

"Taking initiative. I like it! Alright, take off!"

"Ok, buckle up," replied Kai.

"Let's take a stroll through the city and see what the situation is," ordered Angie.

"If there is one," replied Kai.

"Hey, this is important work we're doing here! Now put this on me." She pulled out a leash from one of her portals.

"What's this?"

"It needs to look like I'm your dog."

"You're the boss."

They hit the major spots in town. The market square, a couple bars, and some other random places to get a variety. So far they didn't see anything suspicious. It was getting late, so they decided to get something to eat. Kain bought an assortment of food that everyone would like. He brought it outside so they could eat without drawing attention. They were about finished eating when a familiar face walked by. It was Eric of all people. He was attempting to chat up a girl that left the restaurant before him. She wasn't responding to his advances, so he gave up. Kai didn't want to draw any attention to him, so he continued eating. His attempt to remain unnoticed failed when Rina spotted him, while she followed Eric out of the restaurant with Tuco.

"If it isn't Kai," declared Rina with her arms crossed.

"Rina, how are things?"

"You know, on the run from the Assassins from going AWOL."

"How's that working for you?"

"It's been tough. But we're making it somehow." She sat down next to him looking depressed.

"You're not mad at me?"

"Hey we were only following Nice's orders."

"Eric's the only mad one here," added Tuco. He pointed at Eric who started charging Kai.

"I got this, Kain." He sprung to his feet and drew his sword.

He poured an ice potion on Cheri. Eric started off with a swift kick that struck Kai in the ribs. Someone had been practicing because his speed had increased. He then rolled underneath Kai's sword swing and attempted to stab him in the back with a throwing knife. Kai just managed to block it. He thrust his sword into the ground and froze a small area around him. Now, he no longer had a speed disadvantage. Slipping around and almost falling, Eric started to grow frustrated. Kai tiptoed on the ice and shot an icicle from his sword swing. Eric desperately dove out of the way and threw a throwing knife, which exploded in front of Kai's face into a blinding flash. Now that he couldn't see, the ice was a big problem for Kai. He felt a couple knives sink into both his legs and arms. After falling to the icy covered concrete, he heard a police siren.

"Drop your weapons and put your hands up! You two, on the ground!" said the officer over the loud speaker. A while later the two Assassins found themselves in an overnight jail cell. They were lucky they only had to spend one night, considering one of them might have ended up dead.

"I finally got you," said Eric feeling proud of himself.

"You really did. Good job."

"Thanks."

"What was that exploding knife?"

"Something I'd been working on. I need something that doesn't kill now that I'm not an Assassin."

"Smart. So what are you guys going to do know?" Kai felt bad for Eric.

"We haven't figured it out yet. But we'll figure it out together."

"Why not come back with us?"

"But we betrayed you."

"Was it your idea?"

"No, but —"

"That's good enough for me."

"Plus, you three can't kill us all! Ha-ha."

"Ha. You're crazy. I'll see what the others think."

"You do that. I'm going to try and recover from the knife wounds." He slowly laid down in order to go easy on his wounds.

Cullen and the rest of the team at the base were on high alert when they saw two ships coming in for a landing. Everyone looked ready for war. Kai had to calm them all down and quickly explain what had happened on Sutok.

"I'm glad you didn't decide to kill them," said Cullen with relief.

"What's with having only this guy as backup?" asked Eric, who pointed at Kain.

"Be careful, he's almost as good as me." Cullen warned Eric by pointing his finger.

"I'll believe it when I see it."

"This one has all the confidence in the world!" replied Kain, throwing up his arms.

"Anyways, everything checks out on Sutok," reported Angie.

"Good job, I think Sateer is almost done with her ship," replied Cullen. "Why don't you guys get settled in back at your old rooms?"

"Thanks Cullen. We appreciate it," said Rina.

"Yeah, don't hesitate to ask if you need any medical assistance," added Tuco.

"I'll remember that," replied Cullen. He stretched his arms and went towards his room. "I need a nap. Almost had to defend my home."

"Can we finally get this thing going?" asked Angie.

"Well the Arrow looks better than ever," replied Sateer.

"So what's the plan?" asked Akiko.

"The transport ship is going to be piloted by Sateer with Cullen as her guard. The Talon, with Stacey and Rago, and the Razor, with Tuco, Rina, and Eric, are going to wait just outside the atmosphere to cover our escape if need be. Cam, Kai, Sera, Kain, and Len are going to be on the ground keeping watch as the transport lands. Both the Sprinter and the Arrow will be used by those on the ground," explained Fang, as he paced around the common room. "Any questions?"

"Is there really a chance of running into any problems?" asked Jeff.

"The border patrol might be suspicious of us and decide to request a check of our ship."

"What if that happens?"

"We hope that he doesn't ask to look inside all of our storage containers."

"Can anything else get in our way?"

"Ultimately, we can't just drop off these people if we get caught since they'll just be deported. Therefore, we can't get caught."

"So the cover is just so that we can get ourselves out?"

"Not necessarily. If we're caught before we make the drop, then we can try again under different circumstances. Anything else?"

"What if we run out of food?"

"Shut up, Jeff!"

Once all of the ships took off and entered the atmosphere, they docked with the Arrow. The transport ship for the refugees was too big to dock. A large rectangle went across the center of the Arrow to facilitate the extra ships. It looked like a crude adjustment, but it allowed for quick deployment in case of attack. The dock also had a secondary mode for even quicker deployment. Magnetic nodes were placed on each ship, so that they did not have to physically attach to each other.

Soon the transport ship rendezvoused with the other ships in front of Sutok.

"This is border patrol. Please submit your authentication code for your transport."

"Sending now," replied Sateer.

"I'm going to have to ask you to allow us to board your ship."

"Uh, sure go on right ahead!" Sateer cut the transmission. "Is there something wrong with these codes, dear?"

"They are fine! I think," replied Cullen, as he scratched his head.

"Where did you get them?" she asked with growing frustration.

"Jeff. Why?"

"The spider who only cares about his stomach!?"

"Hey, he's no idiot!" A ring echoed through the ship and Sateer pressed a button to unlock the access hatch.

"Hi, your code says you're carrying a shipment of... frogs? We just came to verify. You can see why, right?" explained the border patrol officer.

"Of course go right ahead," said Sateer with a smile. Cullen was ready to jump into action since he had no idea what was in the first few containers in front. The officer opened up one of the cases inside a container and covered his mouth in an attempt not to throw up his lunch.

"It all checks out, we'll let you complete your delivery. Good day and thank you for your cooperation." The officer left in an awful hurry.

"See, Jeff is *the* spider!" said Cullen, as he nudged Sateer on the shoulder. She rolled her eyes and laughed as she retook the controls to take the ship in for a landing.

"Oh look! Here they come!" yelled Cam with excitement.

"Your plan must have worked, Jeff," said Sera to her little buddy.

"They were sure to be pulled over with my code, but at least no border patrol will want to go near that ship in the future. And I have all the frogs I'll need for a while!"

"Let's go meet them at the spaceport," added Len.

As the team on the ground headed for the spaceport, a messenger handed a note to Kain. Everyone stared at him with suspicion. He told them he would explain later and they let it go for the moment. Once at the spaceport, they began to help Cullen and

Sateer load up the refugees still inside the containers onto the trucks where they could get out and stretch.

     A few hours later they arrived at the town where they would drop off the refugees. They were all thankful to Cullen and Len for giving them a chance at a better life. Everyone was happy to help. Len assured that the pay would be received in a couple days.
     Sateer called the Talon and Razor to let them know that they could head home once they flew by for visual confirmation.
     "We were lucky today. We should be able to pay our Assassins until we can find another source of income," explained Cullen.
     "What are we going to do for money now?" asked Sateer.
     "That's something we're going to have to figure out, but not today. Today, we can celebrate our accomplishment."
     "That's a good attitude I suppose."
     "There's a letter here for you Cullen," said Kain over the ship's radio.
     "Oh? From who?"
     "Master Flint."

Chapter 15: A New Threat

Cullen and Kain were outside the base talking in private over the recent development concerning Cullen's Master. The cool winter air filled their lungs, but things might get heated over the confusion.

"Why did you call him Master and how do you know him?"

"Because he's my master too," replied Kain.

"How? You weren't trained on the Assassin's planet."

"True, but by some stroke of fate he found my village one day when I was still small. He became friends with my grandma and taught me, since I was going to be the teacher of my village when I grew up. He would stop by during his free time."

"He never told me anything." Cullen felt a little jealous that his Master had another student. "Why did you receive the letter then?"

"Because it's safer to contact you through me."

"Damn him! It's no coincidence Kai is my student. Is it?"

"Afraid not. He was always quite the planner."

"Why do I feel like you knew him more than me?"

"That's not true. You're what, nine years older than me? You spent more time with him. He only visited once in a while."

"Thanks. I guess it makes sense our fight was so close."

"Awe, I went easy on you!"

"We'll have to test that out later! Ha-ha. So let me see that letter." Kain handed over the letter, which Cullen opened and read aloud. "Cullen, if you're ready, travel to Venhinge and speak with Jack at the diner on 2nd St."

"If you're ready? What does that mean?"

"It's on Venhinge, so it can't be good. Well, let's go."

"Just us?"

"Yeah, I don't want to tell the others until I check it out first."

"When are we leaving?"

"Early tomorrow morning."

"Yes! I better get ready!" He immediately ran back to his room, while muttering his list of things to pack. "Ok, I'm going to need a med kit, my combat suit, and Venhingean street clothes. I wonder if Cam will lend me some of her special energy snacks."

"You don't think Stacey will care if we use the Talon, right?" asked Cullen, in a bit of a moral dilemma.

"It should be fine. Let's go already! Senior and Junior pupils out on their first mission together!"

"Don't make it sound lame."

"Sorry." Cullen took off as quietly as he could by keeping his speed nice and slow.

"Have you had any other contact with Master?"

"None, he only gets hand written messages to me. The messenger is different every time. Discreet stuff."

"Yeah, it's not even his hand writing. Looks like we're here."

Venhinge, as the name implies, is the capital planet of the Venhingean Empire. The planet had been inhabited for many millennia, so there were all sorts of old monuments to see. If someone was into history, then this was the place to visit. Even though it was an Empire, things weren't as bad as other places. In terms of the society's general happiness it was far better than the Fulmer Empire. The Venhinge leadership believed in work for all, so everyone at least had basic living conditions. Most barely scraped by and crime was largely overlooked, but again it could be worse. Freedoms were withheld, but a strange sense of security came from it.

"So it looks like the diner is this way," said Kain. He pointed to a spot on his phone's map.

"Ok, let's go straight there. I don't really want to be here for too long."

"I feel the same. Either we're being watched or I'm just nervous." They arrived at the diner. They decided to order a drink to calm them down.

"So do you have a message for me?" The waiter's name tag read, Jack.

"Don't linger for too long, it's not safe." He took the payment for their drinks and went back to work.

"What does the message say?" asked Kain as they left the diner.

"I'm not opening it here. Hasn't that guy been following us?"

"Ever since we got here."

"Let's try to lose him."

Cullen headed in one direction and Kain in another. This way, they could see who the primary target was. Cullen seemed to be the only one who was still being followed. Kain also noticed and circled back in order to followed the mysterious stalker. The stalker did not make any strange moves, it only followed Cullen. The problem was Cullen could not lose the woman, by the looks of it.

"Can I help you?" asked Cullen, as he turned around and stopped.

"Yeah, what are you doing here?" answered the woman.

"That's none of your business. Now get lost."

"Now that's no way to talk to a friend." A glimpse of her face showed from underneath her cloak as she spoke to him, now only a few feet away.

"Vesper. I thought you were dead."

"Dead to the Assassins maybe, but no I'm perfectly fine!"

Cullen couldn't handle how cute she was. The former Assassin, who was the same height and age as he, used to be quite popular. Her shiny and shaggy medium long brown hair shimmered and her slender curves moved with an effortless grace.

As she looked at him with her piercing red eyes, she said, "I'll explain more from your jail cell."

At that moment, he was surrounded by three armed soldiers who arrested him. Soon after, Kain was thrown to the ground near Cullen already in cuffs.

"So you're working for the Venhingeans? Wow, I never would have thought you would work for such —"

"Hey, watch it. So tell me why you're here."

"I don't feel like it."

"It doesn't matter because we opened the note you had on you." She slid it over to him.

"Vesper is on to you. Ah, I should have read it!"

"Too bad. It's over now."

"You should know by now that a cell can't hold me."

"That's why you won't be in a cell for much longer. A grave will be far more secure for someone like you. Before I kill you, I thought you should know that I have a force heading to your base as we speak."

"How did you find me?"

"Don't worry about that." She pulled out her Katar and held it up to his throat. She was about to cut into his neck, when an explosion rocked the room.

"Time to go! Thanks for the warning! Oh by the way. You look better than ever." He stuck his tongue out before going into stealth.

"How was my timing," asked Kain, while running behind Cullen in stealth.

"Great, we have to warn the others." Cullen activated All's Eye. "Get ready for a fight. I don't know how many are coming. I'm not sure how many will be Assassins. We're dealing with the Venhingeans."

"You heard him. We have to be ready!" commanded Fang.

It was late at night and everyone was sleeping already. They weren't used to emergency situations like this, so they were moving slower than usual. Stacey didn't bother changing out of her pajamas. She rushed over to the terminal and asked Cullen to fire up the advanced scanners as soon as he warped in front of the planet. A few minutes later he replied and told her there were two large battleships ready to fire on the base.

"You have to call for support from your Assassins right now!" yelled Stacey, in desperation over the transmission.

"Right, this is an emergency." He switched over to a clear channel and called the pilot in charge of the fleet. "Hi this is Cullen. I need you to warp to my coordinates as fast as you can. We're under attack by two battleships. Bring all the firepower you've got!"

"You got it, sir. We'll be there in no time."

"Stacey, try to think of something. How do we repel the first attack?"

"Ask Shippie to begin 'Assault Mode'. They won't be able to ignore you. And switch her to auto-pilot while you're at it."

"You heard her, Shippie!" Cullen was not sure how he felt about the sound of Assault Mode.

"Certainly," replied Shippie as the ship really powered up and shot right at the nearest battleship.

Two missiles were fired at each of the battleships and they were forced to stop charging their cannons. Instead a few fighters were dispatched to destroy the Talon. The auto-pilot was really top notch because the human pilots couldn't keep up. All the while, Cullen and Kain were screaming their heads off due to the insane maneuvers they were unaccustomed to. Every time the two battleships starting charging their cannons, missiles flew at them forcing them to concentrate power on their shields. The process repeated a few times.

An Assassin battleship and a large number of fighters warped into the picture a while later. Cullen and Kain jumped for joy and didn't have the urge to pass out from screaming anymore. Once the fighters joined in, they slowly chipped away at the constant flow of Venhingean fighters coming out of the battleships. Soon they stopped, though it cost a good number of Assassin ships. The Assassin battleship was able to destroy one Venhingean battleship before being disabled by the remaining one. This gave Cullen a chance to dock with the remaining battleship and take it over.

"The ground forces are here!" yelled Fang as he gave the order to attack.

Kai was able to take down one of the ships with his wind attack from his sword. That left two ships and whoever survived the crash. Fang told everyone to not kill anyone, but Kai was not in the mood of letting intruders get away with their lives tonight.

Kai decided to go and finish off the survivors of the crash that he caused. Once he made it, he saw five soldiers trying to pull out someone who was trapped in the wreckage. They fired at him upon sight and he answered with all his might. He even killed the injured ones from the crash. He didn't take pleasure in killing them, but he felt more secure now that they were gone. By the time he arrived the attacking forces were whittled down to just a few. The rest were tied up by Sera's infinite chains or stunned by Rago's electricity. Kai killed the ones who were left right in front of everyone.

"Why did you do that? I could have knocked them out!" yelled Cam. She felt disappointed in her friend.

"A few less for you to deal with."

"This isn't like you. What happened?" added Sera.

"No one complained when I killed Nice." Everyone stood in silence.

"I don't see any flaws in his reasoning. As long as his motive has justice in mind, I don't see a problem," explained Fang.

"You told us not to kill!" replied Cam.

"That's what Cullen wants."

"A soldier has to kill sometimes. That's the way of the world. I don't see a difference for an Assassin," noted Len.

"Well said," added Vesper. She walked out of the forest with her Katar already drawn.

"Looks like we have the leader," stated Sera.

"Very perceptive of you girl. Where's Cullen?"

"Not telling."

"You won't live to see him," said Kai in a threatening tone. His sword was ready to taste more blood.

"She looks tough, we need to work together," said Sera who also readied Jeff. She activated All's Eye.

Cam closed in along with her other two teammates in a V-shaped formation with her in the middle. She went straight for Vesper with her best thrust, which was gracefully dodged. Once the thrust reached completion, Cam rolled forward so that Kai's horizontal wind slice would pass right over her. As soon as Vesper dodged the slash a chain whizzed right passed her face. Now the first step of their attack plan was complete. Sera anchored the thrown scythe to the ground and moved to the right in order to force her opponent to jump up. Once she was in the air, Kai came down with a mighty vertical slash that slammed Vesper's katar.

She showed an impressed smile before breaking with Kai's sword. "Not bad! You kids are a cut above the rest. But now it's my turn." She began a technique that would destroy the young Assassins, but before it could be completed someone had something to say.

"Excuse me, but should you be using that on some kids? Come now, why don't you fight someone close to your caliber?" said Len, completely interrupting her attack.

"If you think you can handle it, then I'll let you sub in!"

"I appreciate it."

"Len, what are you doing!?" yelled Cam

"Who's the soldier here?"

Cam seemed to calm down a little, but she still bit her fingernails. He simply drew his pistol and waited for her to attack. Her attack from what he could see enhanced her speed in order to deliver a powerful jab with her katar. That's all he needed to know. She took off with incredible speed, just as he expected. He made thee carefully placed shots. One shot to the left, then the right, then the middle, exactly in that order. When his attacker appeared before him, her katar stopped in front of his face. The others gasped as they witnessed her die as she fell to the ground. She was covered in three wounds. One on her chest near her left lung, the other in her heart, and the other on her neck.

"How did you do that!?" howled Fang.

"When you get as many Assassins coming after you as I have, you learn how to read their techniques."

"We could have taken him," scoffed Sera.

"Glory hound," pouted Cam.

"It looks like Kain and Cullen are done too." added Cheri. Her All's Eye was still active.

"Looks like you guys wrapped things up nicely. Kai, did you kill these soldiers?" asked Cullen.

"Yes," replied Kai with an unwavering stare.

"I think we should wait to go after the Venhinge directly for a while. Vesper was surprisingly strong. She must have been around my level."

"I agree, she had a few tricks up her sleeve as well," added Kain.

"Good thing I was here to take care of her," declared Len, feeling impressed with himself.

"Thanks. I don't think my students could have taken her, even together."

"See, I told you guys she was trouble. I'm sorry to say that there's more to her and her group."

"What is it, Len?" asked Cullen, looking concerned.

"She worked directly for the Emperor's elite fighting force. They're a mixed bag of Assassin Hunters and rouge Assassins. Not the kind to take lightly."

"How do you know all this?"

"I was an Assassin Hunter for the Free Legion, except we didn't call ourselves that. We were more of a deterrent."

"You merely forced them to abandon their target."

"Exactly. Now do you see why I've been wanted for so long?"

"Yeah. Also if you killed an Assassin, then that would be on your record."

"Anyway, I'm sure the Fulmer have a similar force."

"Any idea how large the Venhinge force is?"

"Large enough to cause problems for us."

"This is bad. They already know our location," added Fang with urgency. "I know! If we invite your conscripts to stay on the planet, we can bolster our security."

"I agree, it's a sound plan Cullen," said Sera who examined Vesper's body. "Do they always wear this uniform, Len?"

"No, but they should have something like a badge so they could prove their status throughout the Empire."

"She has a pin." Sera threw it over to Len.

"Yeah, this looks like some kind of identification." He then handed it to Cullen.

"Hmm. I want everyone to remember what this pin looks like and keep a look out for it. That's all for now. I'll call over the conscripts. Take a good rest everyone. Oh, Kai, could you come here for a second?"

"Yes?" Kai was curious as to where this conversation would go.

"Tell me why you disregarded my orders and killed those soldiers." He looked at Kai eagerly for his answer.

"To protect what we've built."

"Protect. You know Kai, I think that you care the most for everything we've done up until now. I appreciate that, but don't let it change who you are. I don't see a problem with you choosing who you kill as long as you keep protection in mind. You hear me?"

"I do. Can I ask you something?"

"Of course!"

"Could we find a way to change how we're killers in the future?"

"I think I get what you're saying. Sometimes I feel like it's in our training."

"That's it!"

"What?"

"You'll see! Trust me! You're going to like this!" Kai had an idea that would set forth a big change in the future.

Chapter 16: A New Way

Kai had holed himself up in his room for nearly a week now. He was up to something and nobody knew what. He talked to Cullen about how Assassin training concentrated on killing. How could killers save people? The only way open was more killing. It was just a matter of who they were killing. This was the wrong way of going about things. There had to be another way. One that came to mind was suppression. Assassin techniques were full of unique ways of killing. If there was a way to fight without killing and still be effective in combat, he would find it. He started by summoning the Tiger Triplets.

"Your power is the power of influence. Is there a way to use it in combat?"

"What do you mean? You want to influence your opponent's mind in combat?" replied Fuu.

"I want to take away their will to fight."

"I can help you read their minds, Rai is the one who dominates the mind, and Sui designs the command."

"I suppose you could design a command of 'calm', 'retreat', or 'forget'" suggested Sui.

"What if I used 'forget'?"

"That would be least damaging, but it could be reversed if someone were to remind the target of what they were supposed to be doing," added Rai.

"How many people can I hit at once?"

"As long as you can hit everyone within the area before they can help the others, you shouldn't have a problem. Remember, if you're going to attack people's minds like this, then you need to stick to weaker commands, so you don't permanently damage their minds. You don't want an epidemic going around do you?"

"Alright! I want to try it on someone right away!"

"One second. My siblings and I will change our form into a scabbard. If you want to activate us, all you have to do is either sheath your sword before attacking or whack someone with the scabbard itself."

"Got it. Now who shall be my prey?" He let out an evil laugh, while he rubbed his hands together.

He walked around the base and caught Rago eating a sandwich in the kitchen. He really seemed to be enjoying it, but that was all about to change. Kai summoned Cheri as quietly as possible. Once he was right next to Rago he snatched the sandwich right out of his mouth. The furious Rago gave chase. Kai took off and pulled out his sword after going around the corner. Once Rago ran by, he poked him with his sword with the command 'forget sandwich' in his mind.

"Huh? What am I doing here? Wasn't I in the kitchen? What was I doing again?"

"You were about to make a sandwich because you were jealous of mine. Don't you remember?" said Kai as he giggled on the inside. He began to eat Rago's sandwich right in front of him to make sure it didn't trigger anything. It didn't.

"Oh yeah, right." He scratched his head and returned to the kitchen.

"You want to explain to me what just happened there?" asked Sera who just came out of stealth. Kai told her what he had been working on and what he tried on Rago in her room.

"Ha-ha, I can't believe you did that to him! You're really something. I'm glad you took your anger in a positive direction." She was so happy that she hugged him and kissed him on the cheek.

"Thanks, I think it's possible to teach others to do this as well. Once I find a way to reproduce it without my relic's power, I can make it accessible to you guys."

"That's great! Just don't use it on me." She giggled and continued her warm embrace.

"Wouldn't dream of it!"

After a couple of hours of relaxing with Sera, Kai went to see Cullen for some advice on how to implement his new power. He found Cullen training with Fang in his wolf form. As he watched the two of them, who have been partners for years already, continue to hone their skills as seriously as day one, he almost felt bad about interrupting them. They were practicing some type of formation for when they were fighting a tougher opponent.

"Excuse me, but can I ask your advice?" The two stopped in their tracks somewhat reluctantly. With their rhythm ruined, a disgruntled Fang ambled away in a mood.

"Sure, it looks like we're taking a break anyway," replied Cullen, wiping the sweat from his brow.

"I came up with a new technique that I need help implementing in battle." Kai explained how it worked and showed him his general idea.

"Hmm, I think what you have is great. I don't think the issue is how to implement, but instead figuring out your limit. How many times can you use this technique?"

"Let me see." He quickly conversed with Fuu in his mind. "I can perform ten slashes of any sword technique."

"You see that puts a huge limit on your power. If I were you, I'd find a clever way to multiply the effects of one attack."

"I don't know what you mean, but I'm sure I can figure something out."

With that helpful piece of advice, Kai had no idea where to start. However he felt confident that it would come to him when he least expected it to. He decided to check on Cam for a while. Most of his spare time was spent with Sera, but Cam was an important teammate of his too.

Once back inside the base, he knocked on her door, but she didn't answer. Luckily, a hungry spider interrupted his giving up on the endeavor of finding her.

"Cam said she wanted to go off planet to grab some parts for some gadget. If you hurry, you might catch her."

"Thanks Jeff." Kai hurried to the spaceport.

He almost didn't make it in time since Cam already started the Talon's engines. After waiving her down, he successfully convinced her to allow him to tag along. During the flight, she told him how Sera informed her about a specialty shop that carried state of the art mechanical parts for a special discounted price on that weekend only. She wondered why Kai was so eager to come with her and he mentioned how they didn't spend enough time together.

Once they arrived at their destination, a giant shopping district on its own ship near one of the Free Worlds, it was only a short walk to the shop. Unfortunately, there was an insanely long line to get in. Apparently, a few other major shops, which usually ran high prices, had major discounts that day as well.

"Hey Cam."

"I hope they don't run out of the parts that I need!"

"Cam."

"Oh, maybe that store might have it if this one doesn't." She finally turned around after receiving a tap on her shoulder. "Yes?"

"Is there a way to transfer relic energy into a device?"

"For what?"

"I want to expand the range of an attack to cover a wide area."

"I have a few ideas that could work. I'll build the device for you, but you need to buy the parts. How does that sound?"

"Sounds great! It looks like we're almost to the front of the line."

Once inside the store, things started looking hopeless. Many of the shelves had been cleared already. Good thing Cam's parts were all very niche, since she was miles above the average craftsmen skill wise. The parts meant for Kai, on the other hand were mostly simpler in nature. Kai was pleased that his bill turned out quite affordable, but Cam basically emptied out her pockets.

"What are you going to build me?"

"I can't tell you that! It'll ruin the surprise!" She giggled and patted him on the back.

After the two returned to their base, they went their separate ways for a while. It would take Cam some time to build both Kai's and her own device. Kai decided to relax and spend time with Sera.

Over at the spaceport, Cullen was in the middle of talking to the captains of the fleet.

"I'm very impressed with your hard work and sacrifice in these past battles. Now I believe it's time for you to build accommodations for yourselves here at the base. Any questions?"

"Yes. On top of basic living quarters and additional space port landing zones, would it be acceptable to also build quick launch pads and various AA countermeasures?" asked a captain of one of the fighter squadrons.

"That's a great idea! If anyone else has any other ideas for additional infrastructure along those lines, then please don't hesitate to do it. Just make sure that your plans don't overlap. If there are no other questions, then you're dismissed."

"I just want to say that even though not all of us believe in your cause, I believe that you are an honorable man. I intend to follow you as long as that remains unchanged," said the captain of one of the battleships.

"Thanks. I appreciate it."

Chapter 17: Trial by Fire

The cool morning chill managed to penetrate the insides of everyone's living quarters. Winter had properly sunken its teeth into Cullen's team as Rago and Stacey both fell ill with a slight fever. One person wasn't hampered by the weather, the inventor at work, Cam. She arrived in front of Kai's room at 8am and discretely knocked on his door in case he was still sleeping.

"Good morning Cam. You seem excited about something," said Kai as he rubbed his eyes.

"I'm done. You want to try it out?" She spoke quietly while bouncing with excitement.

"Sure. I'll meet you outside in a few."

Cam was surprised to see Kai all geared up and ready to go despite having just woken up. He sported his full training gear, which consisted of his favorite hoodie, sweat pants, and a wrap for his sword arm. Cam proceeded to pull out Kai's prototype energy transfer device from her bag.

"So this hockey puck looking device is designed to store approximately 30 percent of your maximum power. It will take whatever energy you want to give it, whether it is relic or your own. All you have to do to charge it is stab your sword into the center where that slot is. You need to give it all you've got when you're charging it or else it won't be as effective. Got it?"

"Yeah," replied Kai. He drew his blade, took a deep breath, and thrust his blade into the puck with all his might. Cam monitored the potency of the relic energy and how much charge the puck received. The results on her tablet showed an output of 50 percent from Kai's end and the potency of the relic energy read at 100 percent. The two of them heard a loud discharge of the excess energy. The shockwave created from the discharge sent them flying back 10 feet.

"Did I break it?" asked Kai once he returned to his feet.

"Don't insult me. That discharge was from the overflow duct that I installed." She dusted herself off.

"That was amazing! How did you do it?"

"Inventor's secret."

"How can I control my power output?" asked Kai, scratching his head.

"Just tell me how much power you want me to produce," replied Cheri, coiled up in his hood.

"What about with the Tiger Triplets?" asked Cam.

"You called?" said Fuu who materialized.

"Kai wants to know if you can control your power output," repeated Cheri.

"I guess if it's just me, you can get one-third of five minutes of influence. So that's like four minutes, right?" replied Fuu, showing her stellar math skills.

"What my stupid little sister is trying to say is you need to use all our combined relic power for a mere five minutes of... Ah my ear! Fuu get off me!" answered the newly materialized Rai now bitten by his little sister.

"Ah, how does that sound Kai?" asked Cam thinking about her new creation.

"Hmm... I think I just need to try it out. I'll figure out the details later. How about breakfast?"

Kai headed for the kitchen, while Cam woke Akiko. Fang, who is not a dog, was eating a bowl of kibble next to Cullen and Sateer. She was cooking enough breakfast for everyone once they were up. Cullen looked like he was having a hard time waking up.

"Morning guys," greeted Kai.

"Thanks for the alarm. Sounded like Cam's invention really works," commented Cullen.

"We still have to test it out, but I feel good about it."

"You better not hypnotize me again," said Rago, as he sat at the table.

"Count me out as well. I need to keep my mind intact," added Stacey wiping off the grease from her forehead. "That smells so good, Sateer!"

"You came just in time. I'm just about finished." replied Sateer as she plated her pancakes. "Can you turn up the volume on the news update Jeff?"

"You got my food too?" He stopped just before pressing the volume button.

"Your jam covered flies are in the fridge." A news announcement clearly followed.

"In today's news, the Free World of Verde continues to suffer from widespread starvation due to lack of supplies. The shortage has been the result of the Venhingean blockade, which has been going on for three months now. In other news the latest communication device from the number one communication device company hits the stores today," announced the news anchor. He went on to show everyone his new phone.

"The communication devices that Cam made us are way better and come with zero service fees," noted Jeff.

"How do you carry your communication device around anyway?" asked Stacey.

"Ahem... So that's terrible how there's not enough food on Verde!" The spider tried to change the subject, since he could only suspend his communication device in the air with his webs.

"Cullen? What do you think?" asked Sateer.

"We could check it out. Need to find a way in," replied Cullen as he finished off his pancake.

"Kain, why don't you take point on this one?" suggested Fang.

"No way! Really? Okay, I'll go pack!" Kain had been eating his breakfast in stealth. Everyone thought he was still sleeping, the same as Akiko and Sera.

Chapter 18: Aiding Verde of the Free Worlds

Sera and Kain borrowed the Talon. Kain wanted to stop right in front of the blockade to look for any weak points in their security. There were only a few entry points to let in only cleared members of the Venhingean. Breaking though the blockade would be highly unadvised. There was also no way of asking for clearance at the checkpoint. Unfortunately, Kain was so excited about his mission that he knew none of this.

"I think we should steal some credentials first," said Sera thinking logically as usual.

"No time, we're running this blockade!" yelled Kain all gung ho.

"That idea would almost certainly result in the destruction of me. I mean you two," replied Shippie. "Locking manual controls and commencing Self Preservation Mode."

"Override code 243," replied Sera.

"Please don't do this!" begged Shippie.

"I believe in Kai's brother," replied Sera, as she nodded reassuringly at Kain.

Meanwhile on a nearby patrol ship, a radar technician noticed an approaching ship. She quickly called over her supervisor to request the activation of the turrets.

"Yes, what is it?" asked the supervisor.

"It looks like a Fulmer fighter of an unknown model is approaching. Permission to fire?"

"Let me take a look. Bring up the video feed. This has to be one of those top secret fighters we've been hearing about. I want to capture it. Let it land and send a team. Use our clearance code."

"Yes sir."

A few minutes went by and Kain was wondering why no one was shooting. Sera felt uneasy, but there was nothing she could do about it at the moment. Shippie sent a message to Stacey just in case. The message almost read like a farewell letter to one's creator.

Once on the surface, the two made contact with the leader of Verde. Verde was a crucial world for the Free Worlds food supply. Most of the planet consisted of farms of all kinds. The soil all over the planet was extremely fertile. The blockade was so impenetrable that the Free Legion spent three months trying to procure enough troops to liberate Verde. Sera assured the President that they would end the invasion.

Kain was about to call Cullen, when he instead received one from Stacey. "What did you do to Shippie? It sent me a message a short while ago sounding all depressed!" shouted Stacey over the communicator.

"Don't worry about it, we're almost back to the ship and I'm sure it's just fine. See just like I said, it's —"

"Gone!? That's it. I'm bringing everyone in the Arrow."

"No! Please don't do that. Cullen trusted me with this mission and if I screw it up, he won't trust me anymore. We'll find the ship and call you immediately after retrieving it. Sound good?"

"Tell her that she can trust me," added Sera to Kain.

"Stacey said she feels more at ease now that you put in your guarantee," replied Kain after hanging up.

They proceeded by investigating the spaceport. Sera asked the manager to see the security feed. Unfortunately, the ship seemed to open up and fly by itself. This was a concerning occurrence, since it meant there could be an Assassin working for the Venhinge Empire. Now, they had no idea who to look for. The spaceport manager pointed out something odd on the video. There was a piece of paper left where the ship used to sit. Lucy picked it up and brought it to Sera.

"I forgot how cute your cat was! So she's your knuckles, right?" commented Sera.

"Thank you, Master feeds me premium cat chow to bring out the sheen in my fur." She walked over to Kain and rubbed up against his leg.

"I only spoil her because she's the best!" replied Kain feeling proud of his partner.

"The note has the signature of the Grimm Repo-er. What do you suppose that means Master?" asked Lucy, as she investigated.

"Repo?" replied Kain, looking at the Spaceport Manager.

"Ah, this makes sense now. The Grimm Repo-er not only repossesses ships whose owners can't make their payments, but he also steals ships for the Venhinge Empire."

"So how do we go about finding this Grimm Repo-er?" asked Sera.

"Finding him isn't the problem. Getting to him is what's difficult. He actually walks around openly, while protected by private security made up of three Assassin Hunters. They get a lot of business since they can fend off Assassin attacks. Since a repo man makes many enemies, it helps to have such skilled security."

"Master, I think you should let me and Jeff handles this," suggested Lucy.

"My fee is one choco-fly. Anything less and I won't be able to release my full power," replied Jeff, acting like some sort of mercenary.

Sera fed him, then he climbed onto Lucy's back.

"We're off," said Lucy, as she galloped away like a horse.

"Hya!" yelled Jeff, as he whipped her with a strand of webbing to go faster.

"They're at the club a couple blocks away!" yelled the store manager.

The club was just like any other club, filled with loud music, drinking, and people looking for a good time. The Grimm Repo-er sat at a booth with a few women serving him drinks and pretending to enjoy his company. Two of the Assassin Hunters were caught up in the festivities including the women and drinks. The one woman Assassin Hunter seemed very uncomfortable at the booth, so she tried to focus on the music with her back to her two stupid partners.

Jeff crawled into the club and climbed along the ceiling all the way to the Repo-er's booth. Lucy was able to walk in along with those who were admitted by the bouncer. She saw that Jeff was already in position above the Repo-er. The female Assassin Hunter looked vulnerable enough.

"Man, I hate going to clubs. All these idiots do is drink and fool around. I'm the only one who ever does any work!" said the female Assassin Hunter to herself, until a strange cat walked up and gave her the cutest little meow. "What are you doing her here kitty? Are you lost? Oh, you must be hungry! Let's go see if the bartender has any milk!" She picked Lucy up and walked off.

Meanwhile, Jeff descended from the ceiling onto the couch at the booth. The three drunken men were too occupied with the women to notice the tarantula. "No baby, the package you're looking for is in my middle pocket. Those are my keys. What? Hey! That spider just took my keys!" yelled the Repo-er.

"Sounds like an Assassin's Weapon. Time to work guys! Hey get off of her already!" said one Assassin Hunter.

"Sorry, which way did the spider go?" asked the other Assassin Hunter.

Jeff scurried along the floor this time, since the keys were too heavy for him to carry on the ceiling. His worst fears could become real on his way out, getting squashed by a boot or stiletto heel. Luckily, he made it outside to the front where Lucy was finishing her saucer of milk. They both decided to continue running just in case. Taking Assassin Hunters lightly could mean trouble for their partners.

A few minutes later, Lucy and Jeff made it back to Sera and Kain. Luckily, Shippie was not restrained in anyway, allowing it to respond to its remote key. It still seemed upset and refused to talk to Kain who apologized many times over. He finally promised to wash and wax it until it felt like its debt was paid.

"I think we should call it a day and check in at a hotel. Jeff is still shaking from almost getting squashed," suggested Sera.

"Good idea. I need to call Cullen and ask him about our next move," replied Kain, as he checked his phone for the nearest hotel. "I brought enough money for a two bed room at a decent place."

"Thanks, I can split the bill with you. Are you alright?"

"I just don't know what to do. That blockade is almost impenetrable. I still don't see why we made it through." Kain felt discouraged.

"They want this luxurious fighter, Master," claimed Lucy.

"She's right, Stacey took her prototype with her before it was mass produced," added Jeff.

"I didn't know you paid attention to that stuff," said Sera.

"You do a lot of research in your spare time. I'm bound to pick up what you hear." Jeff started to feel calmer after relaxing on Sera's shoulder.

"This hotel looks nice enough," said Kain, who walked through the door.

Once inside their room, Sera took a shower, while Kain reported in to Cullen. Jeff went through the mini-fridge dissatisfied at the lack of bugs. Lucy grabbed a small carton of milk and poked a hole in it with her teeth. She poured it into a saucer Kain laid out for her before calling Cullen.

"How's it going?" asked Cullen. It looked like he was visiting with the Assassins at their barracks.

"I've reached an impasse. This blockade only let us through to steal our ship. I don't think we can make it out in one piece. Someone high in the chain of command has a thing for rare ships." replied Kain, with a defeated look.

"Don't worry about it too much. I'm updating your mission. I want you and Sera to stay on Verde and figure out who leads the Assassin Hunter force. You only ran into three, but I need to know how large a threat they pose. Cheer up. You did well. If Shippie fell into enemy hands, it could cause Venhinge and Fulmer to go to war."

"What about the blockade?"

"I'll take care of it."

"So I failed my original mission," replied Kain.

"That's not true, what would Master Flint say?"

"You're right. I won't let you down. Wait! I never told you about the Assassin Hunters!"

"Shippie sent us a full report. Good luck. Now show me what you can do!" Cullen hung up the communicator.

Sateer finished packing everything on Hope's Arrow. Rago and Stacey dropped off their bags in their rooms. Kai sat in his seat near the forward turret. Cam stood on standby in the engine room. Len waited for them to take off, so he could dock his Sprinter just outside the atmosphere. Once everyone was inside the ship and seated, they headed for Centyen.

The world of Centyen is not only the center of the Free World's economy, but the Free Legion docks its fleet there. The Arrow gained clearance to dock at the reception area of the fleet's hub. The enormous hub was where the entire fleet can both refuel and organize. It also connects all the ships through a central column. The column called Free Legion 1 (FL1) could be its own colony, but it only caters to Free Legion officers. Cullen and Sateer checked in at the front desk.

"Hi, I'm Cullen and this is Sateer. Here are my credentials from the Assassin Council." He slid it over to the secretary. It was basically his passport.

"Thank you sir. Just let me authenticate it. One moment," said the secretary. She scanned it and returned it to him. "Mr. Cullen, Admiral Sadie would like to meet with you. Right this way."

They followed her to the main conference room more towards the center of the column. To their surprise, Admiral Sadie along with all the captains of her unit sat waiting for them to take a seat. Once they sat down, someone poured them a glass of water and asked to take their order. Sateer declined, while Cullen ordered a sandwich.

"Thank you for coming, Mr. Cullen. May I ask why you have graced us with your presence?" asked Admiral Sadie.

"I came to discuss the situation on Verde."

"Of course. As I'm sure you know we are trying to gather enough troops for a full assault."

"How are things coming along?" asked Sateer.

"I'm afraid we simply do not have enough troops for a prolonged engagement," replied Admiral Sadie, as she sipped some water.

"Are there any other options at your disposal?" asked Cullen.

Cullen's peanut butter and banana sandwich arrived.

"This is the best we could come up with considering the enormous number of ships." She handed her tablet over to him.

"How about forcing a battle on the ground?"

"Wouldn't they just bomb the surface?"

"And damage the crops? Isn't that why they're there?" replied Sateer.

"That's it! We could break through the blockade and immediately land on the planet surface!"

"That could work. It might be cutting it close, but I can bolster your force with a fighter escort from my Assassins. Would that work with your current forces?" asked Cullen.

"Let's see, we have four battleships each carrying one-hundred fighters." The admiral checked her tablet for the numbers.

"I have one battleship with one-hundred fighters and an additional hundred on external docks for quick response."

"One hundred on external docks?"

"My student is great with ships."

"According to my calculations, this plan has an eighty percent success rate," added one of the captains in the room.

"That's wonderful!" celebrated Sateer, putting her hand on Cullen's shoulder.

"Why don't you relax for the night and I'll contact you tomorrow, hopefully with details on beginning our assault." Admiral Sadie shook their hands and prayed for approval.

Back on Verde, Kain and Sera had just spent the night resting after figuring out where to start searching for the Assassin Hunter commander. They were going to ask around again, but fate had different plans. Sera was picking up breakfast to bring up to the hotel room, when she noticed some peculiar faces. Something seemed fishy about a woman who was asking for information from someone at the front desk. The woman walked away without any new knowledge.

"Are you alright? You seem troubled?" Sera asked the lady at the front desk.

"It's nothing, just those Assassin Hunters. They think they can do what they want just because they're Venhingean dogs. We may be held captive on our own planet, but I'm going to resist any chance I get," replied the lady, holding her head up high.

"You're very brave. If you tell me what happened, I can do something about it." Sera put her hand on hers reassuringly.

"They were asking if any of our guests had a peculiar pet with them. A spider?"

"Thank you. You keep up the good fight now." Sera headed straight for Kain, but someone would not have it.

"Let's capture this Assassin Hunter and squeeze some info out of her," said Jeff, telepathically from her sweater pocket.

"We might lose her if we wait, right?" Sera turned and went out the door. "What does she look like?"

"She's a little taller than you with large framed glasses. Go easier on her. I think she may be reasonable."

They proceeded through the winding streets and side alleys until they eventually caught up with her. She had been questioning a coffee shop. The fact that she also bought a cup of coffee meant she really did not like bothering people. Sera tapped her on the shoulder and told her she knew what she was looking for.

"You know where the spider is?" asked the Assassin Hunter.

"Yeah, he's right here." Sera held up Jeff in her hand.

The Assassin Hunter immediately stood on guard, but Angie took all three of them to another dimension. This was not a pleasant place by any stretch of the imagination. It was a pitch black cave illuminated by a single small torch.

"What are you doing?" asked Sera, still remaining calm.

"You need to interrogate her," replied Angie with a sinister grin.

"I'm not telling you anything!" replied the Assassin Hunter.

"She was going to kill you. You don't know what they can do. Len saved you last time, this is different!" explained Angie.

"I wasn't going to kill you! I was only ready to defend myself!" The Assassin Hunter started to grow anxious.

"Assassin Hunters know how to negate Assassin techniques! Your stealth! Even your weapon! Jeff can't transform to help you!" yelled Angie in rage. "If you die, then our contract will be void. I have a lot of fun with you guys. Now take my other kodachi and sever her hand." The kodachi materialized and fell into Sera's hand.

"This is your demonic corruption," added Jeff.

"If you own it like Cullen, then it won't be a problem," added Angie with another grin.

"Cullen lost his arm," replied Sera in anger.

"He gained power."

"What will I gain?" Sera had to admit that she was intrigued.

"Darkness." Angie blew out the torch. "The kind where you can only hear yourself and nothing else. Someone could be in front of you and there would be no way to find them. It's something that most fear and only few have experienced. Luckily with this power, you can see all."

"What do you want?"

"Extend my contract to your first born child."

"Fine, but you have to protect my child too."

"I can't let my vessel expire prematurely." Angie felt like it was a deal.

"Ok, so how do I become your vessel?"

"I'll take that as a yes," She jumped into Sera and a surge of pure darkness enveloped the 16 year old. She reached the depths of her heart, which was still pure light. Her corruption had failed because Angie changed long ago. Sera taught her how to be who she was without being evil. In this way, a balanced formed inside of Sera. Two beings living off of each other and supporting one another.

"I'm going to leave you here for a while. Unless you want to talk," explained Sera.

"Still not telling you anything!" replied the Assassin Hunter.

"She doesn't realize that this isn't the other dimension?" asked Jeff.

"I took away her sense of perception. We're still in front of the coffee shop," explained Sera.

Darkness, the possession relic power of Angie, takes away someone's senses and simulates eternal darkness. Once a demon relic possesses their host, they gain a new level of access to their relic powers. Similar to Cullen's possession relic power of the Reflecting Vambrace.

"We're taking her back to the hotel room." Sera picked her up and carried her.

"Good work Sera, you didn't hurt anyone!" cheered Jeff.

"Did I ever give you a reason to doubt me?"

"Never."

A few minutes later the two were back at the hotel. Kain was surprised to see the two of them with an unconscious woman. She explained to Kain that they spotted her and had to capture her before she got away. He reluctantly admitted it being a good idea since it seemed to work.

"Do you feel like talking yet?" asked Sera.

"I'm not telling you anything! Do you really think I can't handle a little torture?" replied the Assassin Hunter.

"Sera, come here for a moment," whispered Kain. "Did you check her for a tracker? If she has one, we could use her to bait the other Assassin Hunters."

"Jeff, check her out."

"Got it," replied Jeff, as he crawled all over the captive. She giggled from Jeff's tiny legs. "She does have a tracker, the signal seems stable. They could be on their way as we speak."

"Follow me." Kain picked her up and brought her back to the coffee shop where Sera found her.

"Tell me when you see her partners, Lucy," ordered Kain. All four of them were spread out around the market, waiting to ambush.

"Yes, Master," replied Lucy, while sitting under the table next to Kain's seat.

"Anything yet, Jeff?" asked Sera from a few tables away.

"Not yet. Did you really need to get coffee?" replied Jeff.

"You're eating your fly."

"I'm always eating a fly."

"Two Hunters coming from your left," reported Kain with All's Eye.

"Can you confirm it, Jeff?"

"Those are her partners." He pointed with his front right leg.

The two Assassin Hunters entered the coffee shop to retrieve their partner who was still under the effect of Darkness. They couldn't figure out what was wrong with her, so they brought her back to their headquarters. Kain's team followed them to the modestly sized base.

"Do you think their boss would be in a place like this?" asked Kain.

"Isn't it too small, Master?" replied Lucy.

"We'll waste our time and likely die, if we go in only to find nothing," replied Sera. "If only we could use our stealth."

"They would deactivate it as soon as we got close," added Jeff.

"Cam did give me this small explosive." Sera pulled out a hand sized remote explosive.

"Could we blow up the back wall and run in through the front?" suggested Kain.

"I don't like it, but we need to get in there." Sera went to place the explosive.

A few minutes later, a large explosion destroyed the back half of the building, later followed by fireworks caused by igniting their weapons storage room. Overall the entire building went up in flames all thanks to Cam's small explosive. Soon, all the Hunters exited the building including a wounded Assassin Hunter Commander. The rescue team called him Commander Paul.

"We're under attack. I want you to alert the blockade. Tell them to tighten security," ordered Commander Paul.

Kain's team quickly left the area and called Cullen as they ran back to the hotel.

"How did it go Kain?" asked Cullen after answering the call.

"The name of the Assassin Hunter Commander is Paul. Also the blockade's security level increased."

"It's alright. I'm on my way anyways." Cullen sounded confident, however in the background Kain could barely make out him saying something to Sateer. "Tell them we need to launch now or we won't get another chance."

"I'm sorry for the trouble. We still don't know the best way to fight the Hunters," replied Kain.

"I'll figure it out, just be careful. They may come after you. For now, I want you to try and clear up a spaceport for when we arrive." Cullen hung up.

"Was Sera alright?" asked Kai.

"Of course, she's my best student," replied Fang.

"You're right, plus Kain is there."

"Are you ready to launch?" asked Cheri.

"I'm a little nervous. We're outnumbered." Kai wiped the sweat from his brow.

"I've got a little something up my sleeve kid," added Len. A bunch of suspicious looking pilots were gearing up for something.

"Ready to go Len?" asked Cullen, now finished with his final preparations.

"Of course. Let's go you guys!" Len was followed by the suspicious pilots. "Don't forget to tune into intergalactic radio channel 156.5."

Len took off in his Sprinter followed by eight Chaser Class racers for the blockade on Verde. Once he arrived, he and the other racers lined up to form a starting line. They angled their lights to form an actual line. They all tuned into the radio station that facilitated the race. The announcer updated them on their lap and all other details on their navigation computers. The race was also televised through the video feeds on the racer's ships. Also, the ninth ship only filmed the race by following the racers from the back. The track ran around and through the blockade. Len competed in races like these for large sums of money because of the extreme danger. Racers were constantly shot down, but that made it fun. Some military establishments allowed them to race and even watched the races themselves. Lucky for Len, the Venhingeans loved these kinds of races. The officers even gave their crew a surprise afternoon break to watch the race.

Sometime during the race, Cullen warped in with all five battleships and temporarily jammed the enemy radar to keep all of them from reacting. The closest stations launched around fifty ships, which were quickly disabled. Luckily, Kain's team was able to clear out a spaceport even though it ended up quite far from the capitol.

"What are we going to do about the Hunters?" asked Sera.

"We just have the catch them off guard," replied Fang.

The sound of a dozen pairs of boots filled the hallway just outside the hanger. It was Commander Paul and his top Hunters.

Cullen and the gang took cover as the Hunters started shooting. Sera and Sateer returned fire. Rago couldn't use his techniques either, so he had no choice but to hide as well. They were all pinned down for a while, when more gunfire came from behind the enemy. It was Verde's military coming to join the fight. The Assassin Hunter Commander just barely escaped, but his men were not quite as lucky.

"Took you long enough," said Fang.

"Status?" asked Cullen.

"The allied forces are retaking the capitol," replied the soldier.

"We'll back you up!" added Cam.

"Lead the way!" confirmed Cullen, motioning everyone to follow.

"Finish the race, Len," ordered Sateer.

"Look up at the sky guys!" replied Len, as colorful fireworks lit up the sky. The nonlethal fireworks commemorated the end of the race.

Shortly after, the capitol was liberated and Verde's fleet launched to annihilate the blockade. Stacey and Rago followed to provide support. Len stayed up in space to further harass the enemy, even without any weaponry.

"Shippie, target those turrets," ordered Stacey.

"Please unlock the controls on the turret, Shippie," asked Rago, trying to fiddle with the joystick. Soon after, he heard a click and began engaging ships on their tail.

Len's Sprinter zipped by and jettisoned more fireworks from his cargo bay right in front of a battleship's bridge. The battleship's crew was blinded and awe struck. The crew members who showed enjoyment were immediately shot.

Cullen's Assassin Fighter Squads also provided support by disabling enemy fighter ships. After a short while, the blockade had suffered enough losses to order a full retreat. The Venhingean on the ground were allowed safe passage off the planet. All in all things went according to plan and the people of Verde could start anew.

"How could I ever thank you Cullen?" asked President Jane of Verde. Inside her office sat Cullen and Sateer. The rest were finalizing the evacuation of enemy troops.

"Don't thank me. Sateer is the entire reason why I'm doing this," replied Cullen, patting his girlfriend on the back.

"I only wanted to help. It's what we do," admitted Sateer humbly.

"What do you call yourselves?" asked President Jane, folding her arms.

"We are the..." Sateer looked at Cullen.

"The Fang Guard," announced Fang, as he materialized from Cullen's sheath.

"That's a terrible... Ouch!" started Sateer, until Fang bit her hand.

"Very well, but I cannot let you go empty handed. I propose a partnership. Verde will supply your people with provisions in exchange for your protection," proposed President Jane.

"It's a deal. We promise to provide both constant patrols and one emergency fighter squadron," replied Fang. The President patted Fang on the head and shook hands with Sateer and Cullen.

Back at Fang Guard headquarters, Cullen received a call from Admiral Sadie.

"My men were awe inspired by your heroics today, Cullen."

"I couldn't have done it without your men. Tell them I said thanks. So how can I help you today, Admiral?" replied Cullen with a cup of hot cocoa in his mug.

"I want to hire you as a private contractor for the Free Worlds."

"What does this entail?"

"You provide us with support in our military campaigns against the Venhinge Empire for pay and supplies."

"My counter is that we help when we can and when we see fit. I won't help if I think you are in the wrong. You can pay us if and when we assist you. Is that alright?" Cullen turned serious temporarily.

"Of course! I'll take what I can get. Is our business concluded then?"

"How much for some raw materials for ships? I have a few repairs that need to be done."

"You have your Stacey to perform the repairs, correct? I will send the materials and workers." The Admiral desperately wanted to be in his good graces.

"Thank you very much, Admiral. I'll send you the coordinates."

"I hope to continue our new friendship, Cullen."

Chapter 19: Stacey's Squadron

"Can you hand me that wrench over there, Rago?" asked Stacey, while working on repairs for one of the Assassin pilots.

"This one?" He handed her the wrench.

"These are some beautiful ships. Did you know the designs are a variant of the ancient models? The Assassin Order is very old yet their technology is constantly updated and installed in their old style fighter ships."

"Too bad we have to take them down."

"I'm sure Cullen will reform them. He's not a killer anymore, remember?" She wiped the sweat from her brow as she tuned the fighter ship.

"He's a good man, but there is still a killer in there, right?" Rago crossed his arms.

"I owe him, so watch it!" She started to grow annoyed.

"Fair enough." He noticed the Assassin pilot came to check on his ship.

"Do you need anything, Stacey?" asked the male pilot.

"Can you hop in and start her up?" Stacey got up from underneath the ship and pointed to the cockpit.

The pilot started the engine, which went smoothly. She gave him the thumbs up indicating that he was good and he turned it off again.

"I'll be off then. Thanks, Stacey, it feels even better than before. I was due for a tune up." He waved goodbye and went to tell his friends about her good work.

After lunch, Stacey and Rago went out for a run. While running passed the barracks for pilots they met a large group clamoring about wanting to get their ship tuned or fixed by Stacey as well. She was wondering why she heard her name and approached them. About fourteen pilots asked her to fix their ships and she happily obliged.

Over the next couple weeks she was able to fix their ships and her reputation grew. She enjoyed the recognition, but she was only one mechanic. They didn't have enough money to hire more mechanics, so she decided to select the best pilots to become her elite fighter squadron. All the pilots, which were only two hundred, were to hold a mock dogfight with laser tag recognition software.

"You must enter the airspace for the dogfight within the 10 second window or you will be disqualified. Please stay inside the atmosphere at all times. Have fun and good luck!" explained Stacy, who gave them directions directly to their helmets.

All the fighters hit the throttle at the same time and engaged each other. The laser tag system computed the time for a lock on and the path for the missiles as well as the path of their machine turrets or Gatling guns. None of the pilots were incompetent enough to miss the window for entry. They were mostly used to fighting in space, but they seemed to be managing.

"Stay on my wing and we'll make it out on top. Squad 2, clean up the border of the airspace. Squad 3, support all directly engaged units. The rest of us in, Squad 1, will be the attacking unit. Let's do this!" ordered the Captain for the Red Team.

"You got it, Captain! Luckily, we have the Jackal on our side guys," replied Reddas, his wingman and fellow captain.

"I told you not to call me that. It's Jack!"

"It sounds better. Watch out for their captain. He should have a blue stripe on his hull." Reddas scanned the area.

As the numbers on both sides thinned out, Reddas finally spotted the Blue Team Captain. If they could only take him out, they could win the match.

"They have the bastard wedged in that V formation," reported the captain of Squad 2.

"Try to pressure them from the side. Squad 3, bolster my attack," ordered Jack, not Jackal.

The large force that protected the Blue Team Captain took a heavy hit from the side and was forced to reassemble the formation. Squad 3 spread out and approached with Squad 1. The Blue team's formation had no choice but to break and engage. It was then that Jack went right for the Blue team captain. They were both the top students in basic training. They both were able to break off from the group and really pushed each other to their limits.

Jack had a missile lock, but the Blue Team Captain was able to evade it. This went on for a while and Jack was nearly shot down a few times. Just when Jack thought this stalemate was never going to end, Reddas, long for Red, swooped in and finished off the Blue Team Captain. Too much time had passed and the Red Team had mostly wiped out the Blue Team. The match was over.

"You can't leave your wingman. You know that!" Reddas laughed and returned to his friend's wing.

As they landed, Stacey and the rest of the ground crew applauded the fine display of piloting. Jack and Reddas received pats on the back and the Captain of the Blue Team nodded in approval. Stacey awarded them with a new patch that Cam designed to also be a homing beacon and link to his comms, whether on his ship or personal comm. Stacey wanted to talk to Jack in private, but he insisted that Reddas also be included as his second in command.

"You and your squad mates will have your own line for comms. You also report directly to me, Fang, and Cullen. If we call on you, drop everything because it is an emergency summons. Please pick 25 of your best pilots from your team today. That's 5 flights from A-E. Your flight will be at base, while 1 other flight will covertly be on standby in proximity to Cullen at all times. Sound good?" explained Stacey, writing on a white board.

"May we choose a different paintjob and patch for our Fighter Squadron?" asked Reddas, Fang entered the meeting room.

"We don't need that stuff! Just pay attention. This is an important opportunity —" started Jack, as Fang jumped up and slapped a new patch on both of their flight suits. There was a Grey Wolf, just like Fang, standing proudly in front of a mountain with the moon rising. He most certainly didn't pose in front of a green screen, while Cam took his picture. Also it wasn't a picture, but an artistic rendering of said picture.

"What are our colors, sir?" asked Reddas with anticipation.

"Navy Blue, Dark Grey, and White," replied Fang, wagging his tail.

"Let's go get the painter!" shouted Reddas. Fang agreed and followed him out the door. The room finally regained its serious tone.

"Ahem, I will also outfit your ships with Shippie version 1.1. That will be all. Thank you, Captain Jack."

"Of course. Thank you again for the honor to serve you." He saluted her and left the room with a genuinely ecstatic smile. Stacey caught a glimpse and silently chuckled.

There was a knock on the door and Cam's head peeked into the room. Stacey invited her inside to sit down. Her bags were packed and she had on her Assassin's uniform. Akiko was even more serious than usual. Something was up.

"Can we please borrow a shuttle?" asked Akiko, who landed on Stacey's shoulder.

"Of course. Where are you heading?" She offered her finger for Akiko to perch.

"Cam wants to survey the other side of the planet. I picked up a large mountain range this morning," explained Akiko.

"There could be precious metals and minerals there." Cam seemed rather excited.

"What are you building this time?" asked Stacey, letting Akiko fly back to Cam.

"It's a secret!" replied Cam with a wink. She took the key and headed for the spaceport.

The approach to the mountain range grew so cloudy that visibility became nonexistent. Some sort of interference made it impossible to fly with instruments alone. A few close calls forced her to slow down, but that third close call sliced open a gash in her shuttle's gut. For some reason, a clearing opened as a patch of clouds parted making for a perfect emergency landing zone.

"Something is calling to me. Must be gold!" claimed Cam, hopping out of the totaled shuttle.

"Let me take a quick look," Akiko flew just up ahead. An invisible barrier repelled her, forcing her to the ground.

Cam let Akiko sit on her shoulder this time and both were able to enter. Once through the entrance, a giant city carved inside the mountain took their breath away. It took up the entire mountain. Some ancient civilization must have lived there. Strangely there was no sign of a battle as the city was intact. They made it to the town square, when they were surrounded by 100 Red Squirrel spirits.

"Why have you disturbed our home?" asked the chief squirrel.

"Our ship crashed, great spirit," replied Akiko with a bow.

"What happened here? What is this place?" asked Cam, who also bowed.

"Long ago, we were the weapons of the Assassin Guards who lived in this city. A terrible plague poisoned the planet's air. We were forced to live here inside Mt. Sky where the air was pure, high above the clouds. Unfortunately it was not enough to save us." He pointed to the memorial stone that bore the names of the Assassin Guards and citizens who perished at Mt. Sky.

Cam immediately said a prayer for the souls of the departed. "Thank you for your sacrifice. Now rest in peace, for we will carry your burden now." The prayer honored the fallen Assassins.

"Thank you, young Assassin." The chief and most of the spirits passed on, except for one. A younger Red Squirrel spirit approached Cam and Akiko.

"I see something special in you. It reminds me of my partner. I offer my services as a relic. I will never forgive the Assassins of the New Way. They set out to decimate the Assassin Guard of the now Old Way. My name is Jacob by the way," said the Red Squirrel with a heavy heart.

"I accept, Jacob, but you have to explain yourself. Tell me everything!" replied Cam who sat on the discovery of a lifetime.

"I maintained the Great Library here at Mt. Sky. A treasure trove of ancient knowledge. Also another reason why I refuse to pass on. Walk with me, while I explain my relic power." They started walking to the library.

Jacob's relic power was called Knight. Cam could knight one person to seed Assassin powers to them. They could only acquire a Red Squirrel spirit of the Assassin Guard as a weapon partner. The form would be that of a Greatsword. Not to be confused with a live and tamable talking animal. Jacob's weapon form was a pair of Tonfa.

The Great Library was the largest in all of Rexa, the Assassin Guard's planet. It was a 10 story building with a spiraling stair case located right up the middle. Jacob's partner was Master Mona, 1 of 10 on the Assassin Guard council. The great scholar taught history at the library, while Jacob maintained it. Those days were peaceful until the Assassins of the New Way tore it all down. Cam and Akiko's jaw dropped, when they reached the library.

"Feel free to enjoy all the library has to offer," said Jacob, excited to show off his library.

"This is amazing! I can't believe how good it looks! So clean!" commented Cam.

"When you have nothing but time, you can clean as much as you want!"

Cam spent the next couple days reading all she could about the fall of the Assassin Guard and the rise of the New Way of the present. She also practiced with Jacob in order to master his relic power and weapon form. Akiko surveyed the city and compiled a map with a device that Cam attached to her ankle. Surprisingly, it was a near perfect match with the libraries maps. It turned out to be a strange kind of vacation inside a ghost town of a city.

In summary of what Cam read, the Assassin Guard, with their home world and seat of power on Rexa, took a stance of balance across the universe. They believed in keeping the 3 great powers, The Free Worlds, Fulmer Empire, and Venhinge Empire, in check. The Old Way dictated protection of the innocent to uphold justice. It was believed to have led to over dependence on the Assassin Guard. During the cleansing of the Assassin Bloodline the followers of the New Way wiped the Old Way from existence. Kai's ancestor, Tolas, was one of the Assassin Guard who became a victim of the cleansing. The disease that decimated all the Assassin Guard on Rexa was manmade. Furthermore, all historical records of the Assassin Guard were removed from history, except for the Great Library.

"I want you to keep this place a secret. Only you can return to access the library. You understand, right?" requested Jacob.

"Of course. Now let's get out of here," replied Cam, packing her bags.

"We need to hike down the mountain a bit before we can get a clear signal," added Akiko. "We can't use All's Eye because everyone will know about the library."

"There's a mine shaft that can take us to the base of the mountain. This way!" replied Jacob, who led the way.

www.ingramcontent.com/pod-product-compliance
Lightning Source LLC
Chambersburg PA
CBHW031336060726
47590CB00007B/2499